A
QUEER DEATH
AT
SECRET PEARL

A LESBIAN RETIREMENT
COMMUNITY MYSTERY NOVEL

J.C MORGAN

Dedicated with love
to the original Crystal Sisters:
KK, TC, WF, LT & SN

Chapter One

All That and a U-Haul, Too

Picture it," Dottie exclaimed, holding her hands up to the sky. "An entire city full of lesbians, all waiting for you to get there." Judith sighed. She could always count on Dottie to be overdramatic. "I don't think it's exactly a *city* full of lesbians, Dottie. It's more like a trailer park in redneck country."

"Well, one lesbo's trailer park is another one's manufactured housing community. Potato, tomato, whatever," Dottie replied. "Just think; you can stop by a different gal's house every day to borrow a cup of sugar, watch reruns of *Gentleman Jack,* or have a quick fling."

Judith pursed her lips, unconvinced. "I think most of the women at the park are married or partnered up. And the single ones are probably not interested in romance and sex anymore." Dottie wasn't easily derailed from her mission to help Judith find the retirement setting of her dreams. "Easy solution, sweetcakes. Be patient. They're old, but you're fresh meat. Just wait for a death or break-up, whatever happens first. Then give 'em a little time to grieve, but not too long, or someone else will come along and scoop them up before you get a shot."

While Judith knew her old friend was just trying to be helpful, she had to roll her eyes at Dottie's over-the-top insensitivity. *But let's face it,* Judith thought. *Secret Pearl sounded pretty darned good.* Its website touted it as "a manufactured housing community for lesbians." The tagline read, "you don't have to be a lesbian to live here, but it sure as hell helps."

Fast forward only three months, and Judith had sold her Minnesota veterinary practice to her associate vet, packed up her belongings, and moved to sunny Florida with her menagerie of pets. Onward and upward to the Secret Pearl, a hidden treasure where around two hundred aging lesbians were already making their retirement fantasies come true.

Judith was lucky. A two-bedroom with a lanai facing the lake had just come on the market, and she'd snapped it up at a fair price. Plenty of space for herself and her animal family, affordable enough that she could retire a tad early. Plus, it was hours away by plane from anyone she knew, and that seemed like a bonus.

And today, she'd returned the U-Haul after dropping the last of her things inside the living room of her late-model prefabricated home, nestled in a little-known wooded area of land just outside of Gulfport. The last box she carried through the door was full of books: everything from the *Merck Veterinary Manual* to the latest true crime novel.

"I hope we fit in here," she confided to her parrot, Hannibird Lecter, as he perched on her shoulder leisurely preening himself and shouting random obscenities. He hadn't learned them from her, though, she thought as she tangled a finger in her greying, curly, and chaotic long hair.

Throughout her career, Judith had met many veterinarians who turned into crazy animal people. She'd never intended to follow the same path, but so many pet owners abandoned their pets once they heard the price of medical services. That's how she had come to adopt Hannibird, a ten-year-old male African grey with a vocabulary full of cuss words and an occasional mean streak. Then, she'd adopted three cats over the last few years, making her an official crazy cat lady. She didn't have a long-term partner, but Dottie often reminded her she still had all the pussy she could handle.

Suddenly feeling exhausted, Judith went to sit on her lanai and rest in the bright, early afternoon sunshine.

Just moments after Judith had poured herself some iced tea and cracked open her latest mystery novel, an unfamiliar face appeared in front of her.

"You the new vet?" A red-eyed lady with stick-straight salt and pepper hair stood in front of her, glancing around at the minimal amount of move-in mess. She had warm, beige skin, a curvy build

2

that her flowy dress featured, a floral tattoo from her left shoulder to her elbow, and bright red lipstick.

"Yes, I just finished moving in today! I'm Judith. Nice to meet you." Judith extended her hand, but the woman suddenly grabbed her in a big bear hug and squeezed hard enough that Judith was forced to extricate herself.

"Welcome to the best-kept secret in conservative-as-fuck Florida! We're excited to have some fresh blood in this shark pond. Come on, I'll give you the official tour."

Judith internally resisted following the woman to her golf cart. She *had* come to make friends, but the introvert inside her begged to get back to her novel, pets, and the unfamiliar quiet of her new home.

"Oh, I would, it's just—" Judith started to come up with an excuse.

"Nonsense. I'm not leaving until you get in. You've got sights to see!" Judith knew she'd lost the battle, and stepped into the golf cart. She slipped a travel-size bottle of sunscreen out of her pocket to massage into her lily-white arms and neck. "You're not from around here, are you?" the woman inquired.

"No, I'm from Minneapolis," Judith replied.

"Well, that would explain why you're as pale as the underbelly of a fish. So how in the hell did you end up at Secret Pearl?"

"I've just retired. I came down to Florida on vacation once and fell in love with it, especially after I found out about this community. And if I never see another snowflake, it will be too soon."

"You're in the right place, Judith. Let's see, what's there to tell about me? Well, I like crystals, essential oils, burning sage, and the word 'fuck.' That's a good starting point. Want a lollipop?"

"A lollipop? No, thank you. I'm not much for candy."

"Neither am I, Judith, but I always share my edibles." The woman produced a lollipop from her shirt pocket and stuck it in the side of her mouth. After a long suck, she pulled it out and gestured it toward Judith. "You sure you don't want some? It's Alaskan Thunder Fuck."

"I'm sorry?" Judith nudged the woman's arm away.

"That's the strain. A couple of licks and you'll feel so euphoric, you'll forget you spent the day unpacking! I brought some edibles back with me on my last trip to Colorado. All you have to do is wrap them in plastic bags and then throw in a bar of Irish Spring soap. Then even the trained dogs at the airport can't smell 'em. Works like a charm! Ya know, I could have paid to get a state cannabis card, but I don't want the government sticking their big conservative nose into my business." The woman looked around suspiciously, as though someone was listening in on their conversation.

"Oh, no, no marijuana for me, thanks. I'm more of a wine drinker myself. I have too many pets around the house making strange noises at night to let myself become even more paranoid than usual."

"So you're more of a Donkey Butter lady then, am I right?"

"I'm sorry?" Judith felt silly repeating herself, but was at a loss for words.

"Donkey Butter. It's a strain of Indica. It can help you calm down and mellow out. We can stop by my place on the way back, and I'll get you some candies. You know, just in case. Never let it be said that I don't share my stash."

"No, that's alright. I do appreciate the offer, though. Is this a different lake, or just the opposite side of the same lake?" Judith found an honest question that would hopefully steer the conversation away from cannabis. She hadn't smoked weed since she was in vet school, and she wasn't about to become goofy during her first meet-up with new faces.

"That's the lesser lake. There're two here; both gorgeous. I live just across there." She gestured to some houses across the bend. "Oh, and a word of advice. You see that flamingo ornament hanging from the doorknob? It's Secret Pearl's version of a sock on the door handle. You see a flamingo there, do *not* come a-knockin'. Wait. Is it just me, or did we go in a circle?" The woman backed up her electric golf cart, narrowly avoiding the curb.

"I'm not sure. I wasn't paying any attention. Just enjoying the view, I suppose. You can't grow plants like these in Minnesota, that's for sure. So, is there a lot of, um, flamingo-on-the-doorknob activity that goes on here?" The women turned down a new lane that ended up being a dead end.

"Oh yes, yes. Especially us retired folks. This is the best time of your life to be having sex if you ask me. Everyone here gets along for the most part. Well, now I just have no idea where we are. Usually, my tours are a little more organized than this, Judith. Too much lollipop, I guess!" She gave it a lick for emphasis, and then plopped it back in her mouth. "Did I already show you the visitor center and the clubhouse?"

"No, but you don't have to. I saw them on my tour. I mean, the tour with my realtor. Not the official tour with you, obviously."

"There's a theater room and a gym. There's a dance floor, too, in the event center. And sometimes Elaine puts on some extraordinary events."

"Elaine, who's that?"

"She's basically the social director here. She's very Southern, and I mean that in the nicest possible way. She won't smoke a joint with me either, because she doesn't think it's very ladylike. Can you imagine? In a lesbian community in Florida? She's something else. In fact, there's a mixer going on tonight at the clubhouse. You must come, especially since I can't imagine you already have other plans. If Elaine planned it, everything will be perfect: the cocktails, the music—there's always something surprising going on at the Secret Pearl! Goddammit, I think this golf cart's battery is dying."

"Oh, no! Where can you get it charged up?"

There was nowhere nearby to charge it. But as she helped push the golf cart back, Judith realized she was thankful Florida was so flat. And she learned on the long walk back that this unusual yet somehow charming lady was Cynthia Chen, formerly of Colorado. She was previously married for twenty years, had kids and grandkids, and loved nothing more than smoking weed and dating around.

Cynthia, still struggling to find her sense of direction, directed them back to her house as the sun was starting to set. Cynthia's yard was full of dead plants, overgrown grass, and psychedelic sculptures. In her window were numerous vials of rainbow-colored liquids. Cynthia nodded toward them. "These are my experiments. If you play your cards right, I'll let you try them one day."

Judith was not at all sure she wanted to taste what was inside the murky, dusty containers, but she smiled and nodded gamely just the same as she stepped inside Cynthia's home. The phone buzzed with a frog croaking tone, and Cynthia pushed several buttons before a loud voice boomed over the speakerphone.

"Honey, hello? Cynthia?"

"Oh, hi. Goddammit, where is that button? You're on speakerphone, dear. I'm with my new friend Judith. She just moved in today."

"You sound like you've had one too many lollipops, honey. I saw the U-Haul turning into Secret Pearl while I was on my way to work this morning, and I said to myself, 'Oh, lord, another lesbian is moving in. Don't you have enough lunatics there already?'"

"You're on speakerphone, dear. Say hi to Judith."

"Hi, Judith! Welcome to the lesbo jungle. You'll get used to it after a while."

"Thank you," Judith said, unsure quite how to respond.

"Gotta go. I'll call you later, dear," Cynthia said as she fumbled with a few buttons on the phone. "That was one of my girlfriends, Kathy. Not my favorite, but she's up there. I don't know about you, but monogamy is just not in my blood. No sir, no way." As Cynthia produced a joint and a lighter from her pocket, her phone lit up again. "Oh shit."

"Yeah, I'm still here, Cynthia. Fuck your non-monogamy, Cynthia," said the voice on the speakerphone. Click.

"Well, that *was* my girlfriend! I guess my Thursday nights are suddenly freed up. That lady needs one of my famous weed suppositories so she can calm her ass down." Cynthia took a long drag on the joint and pushed it toward Judith.

"No, thank you," Judith said firmly. "Really. I mean it."

"Has anyone ever told you that you look like a young Lily Tomlin?" Cynthia said with a smile that meant she might consider Judith a good addition to her newly open Thursday nights.

"Yes, actually, I get that quite a lot."

"I think it's your bright blue eyes and toothy grin. I mean that as a compliment! Who doesn't love Lily Tomlin?"

Cynthia dug around in some cluttered drawers, picking up bags of weed and studying their colors, which seemed to correspond to a chart she had with lists of jars of butter and oil, dates, and potencies. "Nope, not you. Ah yes, you! Here's some olive oil I made with Donkey Butter, for you, my Donkey Butter gal!"

I hope to God that nickname doesn't stick, Judith thought to herself. But she took the small jar of oil, if only to end this battle with Cynthia. She could always throw it away once she returned home, she thought. She did want to return home. It had been a big day, and she was ready to curl up in bed with her recently neglected novel.

"Thanks for the tour, Cynthia. I really appreciate the hospitality you've shown to the new 'lunatic' in the asylum here."

"Not at all. Want me to show you the way home? I think you're on the opposite side of the lake from me. I could drive you in the car while the golf cart is getting charged back up."

"No! No, thank you. I'll find the way myself. No time like the present to learn my way around this place. I like to wander, anyway." Judith's legs ached from unpacking all the boxes, but getting lost again would surely be more inconvenient than taking an extended stroll around the pretty lake. She'd had enough adventure for one day.

"Suit yourself. Are you going to come to the mixer? I'll introduce you to everyone. I guess you could say Secret Pearl is full of odd characters. Some of us you'll love right off the bat, and the others…" She paused. "The others, well, I guess they'll give you something to write home about. You'll be saying 'y'all' before you know it. You are absolutely going to love it here, Doc."

Feeling less reassured than she'd been before investing in her place at Secret Pearl, Judith headed back to her house to take a hot shower and think of an excuse to make it a quiet night inside.

Chapter Two

Judith's First Pearl Party

As Judith stood in the mirror, fresh out of the shower, trying to do something with her unruly hair, she heard the doorbell ring. Still wrapped in a towel, she peeked around the corner to see who it was. Cynthia stood outside, in front of the large window in the front. Judith now regretted her failure to purchase curtains before moving here, as Cynthia waved wildly. "Crap," Judith said as she walked toward the front door.

"Time to party, doc! Look, I brought wine, because I'm considerate like that."

"Oh, Cynthia, I'm afraid I can't go. The stress from moving has got me coming down with a cold. I have a fever, and I need to get some rest." Cynthia put the back of her hand to Judith's forehead, where Judith prayed the heat had lingered from her shower.

"It must be boogie fever because you feel fine to me. Put on some clothes, and let's go, girl!" Cynthia made herself quite comfortable on Judith's couch, and Clawdia, Judith's friendliest cat, climbed right onto her lap and started purring. "I'll just wait with my furry friend here until you're ready to go."

Judith sighed inwardly and slinked back to the bathroom. She put on a simple, comfy black dress, realizing she had no idea what kind of a mixer this was, and hadn't noticed what Cynthia had chosen to wear. When she stepped out, Cynthia whistled.

"Wow, Judith. We're going to a mixer in Florida, not the Met Gala."

Judith now realized that Cynthia was in a faded Grateful Dead t-shirt and wearing jeans with paint splotches on them.

"I can change—"

"No, don't. Elaine will be pleased that someone else around here gets dressed up for her events. Usually, she's the only one who puts in the effort." In a matter of moments, Judith was as ready as she would ever be, and Cynthia drove her on a zigzagged, doubling back, where-the-hell-are-we path toward the mixer.

Stereotypes had apparently gotten the better of Judith. What she'd pictured was a room full of dapper, greying butch ladies listening to country music and drinking beer, maybe line dancing. But the mixer was not what she'd expected at all. Some women in attendance were as young as their mid-forties. Others were old enough that this could be their last Secret Pearl event, thought Judith. Butch, femme, and everything in between was comfortably within her view. Twinkly lights and pretty floral centerpieces adorned each table. Across the back wall of the clubhouse was a gorgeous painting of Frida Kahlo, unibrow front and center. Upbeat orchestral music played in the background.

"This event is classy as fuck," Cynthia remarked as they made their way to a table with some open chairs.

And then, Judith saw a woman she instantly identified as Elaine.

Elaine had straight, silvery grey hair cut into a pretty bob. Wearing a shimmery red, off-the-shoulder dress with a black scarf, she almost looked European. It was clear she'd planned the party. She glided elegantly across the floor to meet the unfamiliar face. There were other people milling around, too, but Judith failed to notice any of them. She turned back to Cynthia before Elaine could catch her staring.

"Oh, look, Elaine's heading our way," Cynthia said, unaware that Judith had already intuited this.

"I'm Elaine—Elaine Jones." Elaine had a slow, dripping southern accent, and her pronunciation of Elaine had about four more syllables than Judith expected. Judith wasn't a love-at-first-sight type of person, but she wondered now if that was only because she had never met Elaine.

"Charmed. I'm Judith," she said, as casually as she could muster.

Judith marveled at how the longer she lived, the easier it was to see where things were heading. She couldn't see the future—she was too much of a science devotee to believe in any of that tea leaves type of crap. But her gut feelings were often accurate because, over the years, she had honed them. She would always journal about her instincts and track what turned out correctly and incorrectly.

Tonight, Judith would write in her journal about how Elaine wasn't mesmerized by her—yet. But in due time, she would feel the same way Judith felt right now. She would write about how in a few days, weeks, months from now, Judith would wake up in Elaine's bedroom, tousled and sweaty, tired but happy. She would cover Elaine with her own cozy comforter, Elaine's sweat leaving her too cool under the intensity of the air conditioner. Then Judith would get them both tall glasses of sweet tea. She could see the moment clearly, and she desperately hoped her premonition would turn into reality.

She didn't know if Elaine had a partner, but it didn't matter. Judith would wait, just as Dottie had advised her. The sexual urgency of youth had aged and become more nuanced, like the wine Judith now eagerly awaited. As the urgency faded, it was replaced by something better: finesse. No more were the days of throwing someone up against the bathroom wall at a bar. Instead, there were candles, hours of talk and teasing, massage, music, and surprise. At least, that's what Judith's fantasies told her.

"I'm happy to see that someone else here has some taste, Judith." Elaine smiled and turned her svelte body to face Judith as she handed her a glass of red wine. Judith loved that her Georgia-peach accent seemed to drop consonants at will and turn vowels into an entire event. "You seemed like a Beaujolais kind of girl to me, but if I'm wrong, go on over to the bar and have them make you something else."

"Oh, get over yourself, you antique Cinderella," Cynthia said.

Elaine paid no mind to Cynthia's snide comment, but turned around and carefully stepped onto a little stage while grabbing a microphone from a table.

"Attention, attention. Thank you, ladies of the Secret Pearl, for attending tonight's mixer. We have a special guest tonight, our newest member, Judith! Judith, this is everyone, everyone, this is Judith. Please make sure to introduce yourself before you leave tonight. Let's give our newbie a little toast: to Judith, may she love every moment here as much as we do!" Elaine raised her glass, and Judith raised hers to the toast as well.

"I want to add that we're not here to get drunk tonight, ladies. We're here to *learn* something. I've requested Secret Pearl's own sommelier to give tips on correctly pairing wines with cheeses." Elaine gestured to a buffet table set up with a dozen different kinds of wines and twice as many cheeses.

"A some-of-what?" Cynthia mumbled, her mouth already full of crackers.

"A sommelier. A wine expert," Elaine answered. "She's going to add a touch of class to our get-together tonight. Helen, the floor is yours."

Helen, an older resident, walked to the mini-stage and took the microphone into her hands. She had dark hair cut close to her scalp, and warm dark skin that glowed from underneath her tailored, red suit. But the ladies were already losing focus. A woman who would soon be introduced to Judith as Brenda produced a can of Cheez Whiz from her backpack and addressed the crowd of women before Helen could even start to speak.

"I never leave home without this stuff. Nectar of the gods. Hey Helen! Which adult beverage goes best with Cheez Whiz? Bud Light, you say?" Brenda squirted some of the canned cheese directly into her mouth before swishing it around with the beer. Judith walked over to better hear Helen, who was doing her best to muddle through her presentation.

"Save your tannins for something aged like a mature cheddar. If you're having sweet wine, try something a bit funkier like blue cheese, or a creamy cheese like brie. But if I were you, I'd have brie with a nice oaky Chardonnay. Just a personal preference. Tammy, no, Boone's Farm Strawberry Hill isn't the perfect complement to American cheese. Martha, you'd better get that ice cube out of your Silver Oak. I may be old, but I can still see you, and I know where you live."

Eventually, Helen gave up and handed the microphone back to Elaine. Elaine sighed and said to Judith, "Well, I tried."

"If it's any consolation, this is the most fun I've had at a party in a really long time. Of course, I don't attend many parties," Judith chuckled, as Elaine stepped down off the stage. Elaine laughed.

"Thanks. It *is* some consolation. Now, let's go meet everyone." Elaine grabbed Judith's hand and led her toward a concentrated area of partygoers. Judith practically floated behind her, feeling confident she'd moved to precisely the right place to retire.

"Brenda, take a break from gulping Cheez Whiz, won't you, and meet our newest resident! This is Judith. I don't know her and I already like her. She's a...now, what exactly is it that you do, Judith?"

"I'm a veterinarian at a clinic in Minneapolis. Well, as of a few weeks ago I was. I'm retired now. But I practiced for many years, and now I just have my cats and a potty-mouthed parrot to keep me company."

"That's the most fucking amazing thing I've ever heard before. I love vets. People who take care of animals are the salt of the earth."

"Brenda, language," Elaine said, with a roll of her eyes.

"Sorry, that's the most fucking amazing thing I've ever heard. Hate it when I end a goddamn sentence with a preposition, don't you, Elaine?"

"Brenda is the Secret Pearl's, um, how should I put this? Brenda is the most active dater in our community. She's a legal consultant now that's she's semi-retired. But she used to be a big-time attorney. Her career was just as fast-paced as, well, everything else about her," Elaine disclosed.

"Yes, I'm the resident slut is what darling Elaine is too proper to say. I used to be a lawyer, and I've got the fucking vocabulary to prove it!" Brenda smiled jovially. She had short, curly hair and a smile that lit up her whole face. She was eyeing the room full of women. "Who shall I bring home tonight, Judith? Elaine is pretty, but she's not my type. I like athletes. They have so much endurance, don't you think?"

"Oh, I don't know," Judith said, blushing. Elaine took Judith's hand and guided her away from the awkward questions. "Okay, over there," Elaine said, pointing to an athletic woman with a great tan and wearing a visor. "That's Jo. She's an odd duck, but comes in handy when you least expect it. You didn't hear it from me, but she seems to come from a less-than-legitimate occupation. Maybe I'm just judgmental. And over there is Linda—Linda Abrams. She's older and essentially invincible. We had a break-in a few years back, and she fought the intruder off with a shovel. Yet she always thinks she's dying. I'm surprised to see her out of her sickbed for this event. And there's Wheezer, who defies description. You really have to experience her to understand. Come meet her. Wheezer! Over here."

Elaine guided Judith toward an older lady who exuded a sort of boyish charm and endearing butch energy. She had short grey hair and a mischievous grin, though it wasn't so much of a grin as a smirk.

"Well, what do we have here?" Wheezer was glaring at Judith, but Judith didn't notice because she was distracted by her sultry and deep voice, reminiscent of Kathleen Turner. She sounded like she was from a different era—years of smoking, no doubt.

"Wheezer, this is Judith. Let's welcome her to Secret Pearl. Wheezer is outspoken, but once you get to know her, you'll love her."

"Don't count on it, sweetie. I didn't move here to make friends, and I sure as hell hope you didn't either."

"Technically, I moved here to retire."

"Wow, retired at your age! With that kind of money, I'd have supposed you could afford a dress that was a bit more flattering."

Elaine tucked Judith's hand into her elbow crease and led her away. "Don't take her seriously. She'll come around. She's just got a thick outer shell, Judith. That might be enough meet and greets for one night. Shall we go taste some more wine?"

Elaine and Judith meandered back to the table full of wines and cheeses.

"So, first impressions. What do you think of the Pearl so far?" Elaine sipped from her glass of cabernet and tasted a square of gruyere. It occurred to Judith that Elaine had actually paid attention to Helen's wine-pairing advice.

"It's nice that I don't have to come out to everyone I meet. I already feel at home in that way. But with all this good weather, I think I'm going to miss having snowstorms as an excuse to ignore social activities and curl up with a good mystery. Don't get me wrong, I won't miss the snow for any other reason. There's nothing more irritating than getting up early to shovel and scrape ice off my car's windshield before work. And now that I'm free of both snow and work, I hope I don't get into any trouble." Judith winked at Elaine before realizing she had probably imbibed enough wine for one evening.

"There's plenty of trouble to get into at the Secret Pearl with all these gals being queer as a three-dollar bill. That's why I had to start planning parties—to keep myself busy. I'm retired, too. Divorced and retired; footloose and fancy-free for once in my life!" Judith could have listened to Elaine's sticky-sweet accent forever. She nearly got so lost in the sound of it that she neglected to comprehend the information contained in Elaine's words. There was a long pause.

"Sorry, Elaine, I just find your accent so delightful. Where are you from?"

"Berkeley Lake, Georgia, so I'm not quite as country as I sound. It's right outside of Atlanta. I went to Duke for college, majored in engineering, and knew I could never move back to Atlanta again. I needed to be near the water. I'm part fish, you know."

"Well, if you're a fish, and I'm still technically licensed, I can do your physicals—at least for the next six months until my DVM license expires." Now Judith was *absolutely* sure she'd had enough wine.

Suddenly, a scream came from the other end of the room. Jo and Wheezer were standing outside the bathroom door, and Jo was gesticulating wildly.

"Betty's dead!" Jo screeched. "I'm not joking! Come see for yourself!"

Elaine guided Judith toward the scene, where Wheezer looked more displeased than surprised.

Words tumbled out of Jo, one after the other. "I picked the lock for Wheezer, who was hopping up and down, waiting for the bathroom. You know how she gets. I just happened to have my lock picking set with me, so I thought I'd help her out. It'd been occupied for a while, believe me, over twenty minutes. Oh my God, I can't believe she's dead!"

"Must have been one hell of a dump," Wheezer said, pouring herself some more wine.

Chapter Three

Cheese It, the Cops

Of course, we have a new resident move in, and everything goes straight to hell, Elaine thought to herself. Betty had kicked the bucket, and now everyone had seen her naked corpse on the toilet. *What a way to go. What a nightmare.*

The women stood there, some gossiping about the tattoo of an iguana on Betty's thigh they never knew she had, others horrified merely from the visceral nearness of death. It was the worst ending to a party since Elaine's commitment ceremony. That's when Elaine's new bride had too much to drink and announced to everyone within earshot that she wanted to have an open relationship. And then following up her outburst with an equally embarrassing confession about being in debt to loan sharks from her gambling habit.

It was a wonder Elaine still liked parties at all.

Elaine called the cops and then, a minute later, she decided to alert the local Catholic church to the death. After all, Betty had gone to mass on Easter, as Elaine recalled. Elaine always felt like she was the den mother at Secret Pearl—and a rather unappreciated one at that. Meanwhile, everyone raised a glass to Betty, but otherwise, the party had resumed and Elaine was the only one taking action. The cops didn't sound concerned. They knew Secret Pearl was mostly made up of retirees, so a death was not a shocking event, to say the least. They didn't even seem sure it required police intervention.

"Officer, it was just the look on her face. It, well, it wasn't natural!"

The phone trembled slightly in Elaine's hand as she spoke with the police. She was traumatized by what she had witnessed. Betty was just sitting there, naked on the toilet, with a look of supernatural astonishment on her face, somewhere on the spectrum between horror and delight.

"Everyone liked Betty, Officer. It was impossible not to. She was one of our younger residents and an astonishing baker. It made her extremely popular around here, honestly. Who can resist a perfect flaky almond croissant?" Elaine chuckled to herself.

"Yes, ma'am. But did she have any enemies, either here or elsewhere?"

"Why, I'd be the last to know. We weren't awfully close. I know she had some family up in north Florida. I'll look up their information and call them in a few minutes, but Betty really did keep mostly to herself."

"We'll send an officer out right away to take statements from everyone, and we'll let the coroner's office know, too. I appreciate the call."

Violent crime in Florida had been diminishing over the past couple of decades, Elaine knew, but the police were always busy chasing one suspect or another. A probable natural death wouldn't be at the top of their list.

Elaine tried to comfort some of the other residents who were visibly shaken. Before long, a priest and several nuns came by to give last rites. But being too late, they offered prayers they referred to as *The Office at the Parting of the Soul From the Body.*

"How did you get here so fast? You beat the cops," Elaine said to the young priest.

"The Lord works in mysterious ways," he said with a grin.

"Did the Lord give you a private jet? I was on the phone with you not five minutes ago!"

"To be honest, ma'am, the nuns and I were taking a brief reprieve from our calling at the bar just down the road from here." Elaine smiled at the priest and gestured as if she were zipping her lips.

Linda's hypochondria must have flared up as it so often did, because she stretched herself across three chairs and flagged the priest over.

"Father, could you just do mine too, while you're here?"

"Your what?"

"My last rites. I have a debilitating, sometimes-fatal condition, and I could go at any minute, Father." Linda lifted the back of her hand to her forehead and closed her eyes, as if she were seriously ill and not shotgunning Cheez Whiz just twenty minutes ago with Brenda.

18

"My, my. What is your ailment?"

"I'm allergic to shellfish," Linda said, a bit sheepishly.

"That's not a fatal condition, my child," the priest said patiently, with concern in his voice. Linda shot up from her makeshift bed, surprising the priest with her energy.

"It most certainly is in Florida! They put shrimp in everything here. Every time I dine at a restaurant, I'm taking my life into my own hands. Can't you do it just to be safe? Or to save yourself a trip when something does happen in the next couple of weeks?"

The priest sighed. "I'll do an anointing of the sick. You just need to come to confession as soon as you can, dear. I think you'll feel better, less anxious."

"Shhh, just bless me." Linda crossed herself and laid back down in resignation.

"Ignore her, Father," Elaine said. "Not too long ago, she beat an intruder away with a shovel. She's as healthy as a horse."

"Is there any other way we can serve you women in your time of grief?" The priest addressed everyone, and Brenda's hand was first in the air.

"Yes, please. Could you have the nun with red hair give me a sponge bath?" Brenda bit her lip and smiled. "Oh, don't give me that look, Elaine. I saw everyone in here turn to check out her hourglass figure," Brenda whispered.

"A sponge bath? No, no, that's not part of our regimen. We mean spiritually."

The nun headed over to Brenda, sitting next to her gently, placing her arm around her, and smiling in such a way that gave everyone the impression she thought Brenda was suffering from dementia. "I'm here to live out the word of God, so if you need a listening ear, I can be that for you."

"I do, Sister. Betty and I were close, and I am just devastated. The only thing that could possibly make me feel better is if you come over and hold me until I fall asleep. You don't even have to touch me. You could just recite the Ten Commandments, or something, maybe make up some new ones. You can command me to do whatever you want." *Brenda is shameless*, thought Elaine.

"I'm sorry, ma'am. I'm not sure that's a good idea." The nun looked around the room helplessly. "Will someone make sure this woman gets safely to bed tonight?"

"Yes. Who will volunteer to tuck me in?" Brenda shot Judith a wink. There weren't any takers, but that didn't seem to bother Brenda in the slightest.

"I'm afraid we'd best be on our way," the priest said to Elaine, slipping away after offering a brief prayer for Betty.

Brenda snuck over and, when she believed no one was within earshot, whispered in the priest's ear, "I'll buy you a drink if you tuck me in."

"I'll see you in confession, Ms. Williams." Naturally, the priest knew Brenda; Brenda made it a point to know everyone in town.

As the priest and nuns made their way for the door, Elaine thanked them for their time and apologized, yet again, for Brenda. Through the doorway, she could see the cops arriving.

"Thank goodness you're here! We've been careful not to touch anything. Betty, the woman who died, she's waiting for you in the bathroom."

After identifying themselves as Officers Hank and Jeremy, one pulled out the report that had been made and started speaking as the other man jotted down his words. "Eleven o'clock on Friday night. Death under suspicious circumstances in Pinellas County. Secret Pearl. Betty has died. And I'm sorry, miss, but you didn't give her last name on the phone."

"Betty Black," Elaine said, remembering Judith was on the other side of the room, lost in the chaos. "Anything you need, officers, I'm happy to help. I'm just going to go talk to my friend for a moment."

Elaine rushed across the room to find Judith sitting calmly, flipping through an old issue of National Geographic. "Judith, what a night! I can't believe it. Usually, the ladies of the Secret Pearl are begging to curl up together in a great big lesbian housewarming puppy pile. But a potential murder? I never thought it could happen here. I do hope you'll stay. Do you want me to walk you home?"

"That would be lovely, Elaine." Judith stood up and stretched. "Who was Betty anyway?"

"You didn't get the chance to meet her, but she lives right across the street from you. I'm not stalking you, I promise—you just bought the only unit available right now."

Sensing that the women were eager to get home, one officer shouted through his cupped hands, "No one goes anywhere until we're able to collect statements from all of you. Sorry, ladies, I know it's late, but it doesn't matter if this takes a couple of hours or a couple of weeks. We need all of you here."

Brenda stomped her right foot on the ground. "Ladies! You better get your statements in order, and I mean fast! A select few of us have a trip planned to Key West in a couple of days, and I am not missing that trip because y'all screwed the pooch. You hear?"

The ladies lined up in a hurry, ready to get home and go to bed, and the police officers set about securing the scene.

Chapter Four

―――――――――●―――――――――

Murder, She Wrote

N ow, let's do this in an orderly fashion," Officer Jeremy said, adjusting his badge. "Who was first on the scene? Who discovered the deceased, Ms. Black?"

"I did," Wheezer and Jo said simultaneously.

"You both did?"

"Stop trying to take credit for something you had almost nothing to do with," Wheezer rasped.

"I opened the door. You see, the door was locked and it was clear somebody had been in there for quite a while. I'm the only one around here who can pick a lock worth a damn, so I helped Wheezer out before she had an accident on the floor," Jo said.

"You can pick a lock? And what did you say your name was?" Officer Hank was furiously writing.

"My name's Jo Medina. I didn't kill her, though; I was just preventing a situation. You know how it is. This clubhouse could use some more bathrooms, that's for sure."

"Look, nobody said anything about someone being killed. We'll take all of your statements separately. Jo, you're first on our list. Elaine, can we use this little conference room to conduct our interviews in private?"

"Sure thing, boys," Elaine said, looking up momentarily from an in-depth conversation with Judith.

Hank, Jeremy, and Jo all filed into the conference room, with worry written all over Jo's face.

"Would you mind emptying out your pockets for us, Jo?"

"If I must." Jo laid out her keys, cell phone, wallet, an entire lock picking set, and a travel-size bottle of lube. She shrugged. "You never know when you're going to need it."

"A lock picking set?"

"No, Officer, I was referring to the lube—just joking around. I'm sorry, I'm nervous."

"Lesbians use lube?" Hank asked, causing his partner to elbow him.

"Yes, we do. And you have to use the right kind. If I'm with someone who has flavored lube, then you'd better believe I'm going to end up with a yeast infection. That's just the way it is. I turned fifty-five, and I just made a decision that wherever I go, the lube goes, too. It's never let me down. Unlike some women I know."

"Thank you, Jo, this has been very, uh, informative. That's all the questions we have for you!" Hank said, clicking his pen and shuffling his papers.

"Jo, sit down. We do have more questions for you," Jeremy said. He glanced over to Hank and shook his head and turned his attention back to Jo. "Hank, erase whatever you wrote down about lube. Now, how well did you know Betty?"

"Oh, not well. Loved her baking, though. I had a bit of a crush on her—like most of the women here. But she was very private, and she didn't come to a lot of these events. Unless there was line dancing. Then she would show up every time."

"And where were you at the time of her death?"

"I've been here at this party since seven in the evening. Haven't left the premises."

"Thanks, Jo. Can you please send in the next in line?" Jo left, and Jeremy leaned over to Hank. "Hank, for God's sake, will you let me ask the questions? You always leave out the most important ones, and then we get in trouble. This time, we're not getting kicked off the case. This time, we're solving it."

Wheezer came through the door only moments later.

"Well, I'm here. Let's get this over with, shall we?"

"Let's start with your name, ma'am."

"Wheezer."

"Wow, were you named after the band?" Hank asked.

Jeremy rolled his eyes and made a gruff shushing motion at his partner. "Shut the hell up, Hank. Alright, what is Wheezer short for?" Jeremy asked, appreciating the willingness of this witness to get right to the heart of the matter.

"Eloisa Martin. I got my nickname because I smoked for an awfully long time. It was the cool thing to do back in the day."

"And were you acquainted with Betty?"

"Acquainted, yes. I'm acquainted with everyone in this place. But that doesn't mean we were friends."

"So, you weren't friends?"

"I don't make many friends, Officer, and I like it that way. I'm too old to put up with people's bullshit anymore, and that includes yours. Any other questions?"

Hank raised his hand as if he were in school. "Me! I have a question. How did you find out that you're a lesbian?"

"Jesus, Hank, would you just keep your damn mouth shut and let me do the talking? Moving on. When you walked into the bathroom tonight, what did you see?"

"Betty. Dead on the toilet. That's about it."

"And how would you describe her?"

"Pants around her ankles, mouth halfway open, fingers clutching a few squares of cheap-ass toilet paper. I screamed, Jo screamed, and then Elaine called you guys. If that's all you have for me, I'd love to get out of here. I have some explaining to do to a certain someone waiting back at my house." Wheezer's scratchy voice seemed to be turning into a growl.

"Oh, so you have a partner?"

"No, just my cat, Pants."

"Did you and Betty get along?"

"You could say we got along. I thought she was kind of flighty and vain, and I told her so. But we didn't have any bad blood. I just speak my mind, is all."

"Did Betty have any enemies that you knew of?"

"No, Betty was a generally nice person—or, as I usually call them, a sucker. She wasn't great with money, but that was her only big failing, as I see it."

"Thank you, Wheezer, this has been helpful. Send in the next witness."

Brenda sat down in front of the two young men with a fresh coat of makeup and some recently sprayed perfume that was slowly seeping throughout the room. Brenda leaned over toward Hank, her bobbling breasts making her low-cut dress look obscene.

"Officer, have we met? I swear, I recognize you."

"No, ma'am, I don't think so." Hank blushed a little at the attention.

"Well, in the spirit of full disclosure and to help solve Betty's murder, I have a confession to make. I'm really more of a part-time lesbian, if you know what I mean. On the weekends, I like to do a little experimenting."

"So, you're a lesbian and a scientist?" Hank asked, impressed. Officer Jeremy shook his head and rubbed his temples.

"No, sweetie. I mean I'm a little bisexual. Just a tiny bit. Don't tell the other girls. It'll be our little secret, okay?"

"Yes, that's fine," Jeremy said, clearly annoyed and checking his watch, wondering if he'd ever get home. "So, how familiar were you with Betty?"

"Oh, very," Brenda said with a smile. "Very." Her eyebrows curled up into a devilish shape.

"Alright, define your relationship for us."

"Every once in a while, I would text her in the middle of the night, and she'd head over to my place. So, it wasn't like we were partners; it was more like we were fuck buddies—pardon my French. I guess the polite thing to say is friends with benefits. Sometimes she would text me in the middle of the night. She was younger and pretty as a peach. Creamy skin, she always smelled like apples. I'm going to guess she was about a D-cup. Petite though. Kept in great shape. A big fan of oral, at least when I was between her legs. Total screamer. Can't have the windows open when you're going down on that one!"

"That's—that's plenty," Jeremy said. Hank looked at Jeremy for clues as to what he should write down from Brenda's last answer, and Jeremy just shrugged. "Did you two have a falling out?"

"Oh, no. What's to argue about? We had the perfect arrangement. When we were both single, or at least theoretically single, we'd meet up for several hours of no-strings-attached sex! Sometimes it was several days. For a while, she got into Tantra—"

Jeremy cut Brenda off again.

"Great, great. Do you know of anyone who disliked Betty?"

"Oh, just Wheezer. But then again, she hates everyone. Even me, if you can believe that."

"Thanks, Brenda. You've been very," the officer paused before he thought of the right word, "thorough. Send in whoever's next."

Not a minute later, Cynthia walked in and sat down smelling of patchouli and looking a bit dazed.

"Look, I'm going to level with you. I don't like cops. I'm going to get my medical card soon, cross my heart and hope to die. So don't even get on my ass about this." Hank and Jeremy exchanged looks. So many ladies in this resort, and not a sane person to be found.

"Noted. Please state your name."

"Cynthia Chen."

"In your own words, please tell us about what happened tonight."

"I brought the newest resident at Secret Pearl to the mixer that Elaine planned. It might have been a mistake. I kept getting lost. Once we got to the party, Helen was supposed to educate us common folk about how to pair cheese with wine. Everyone here likes line dancing and beer, except the person planning our events. Go figure. But then, that's where things get crazy. Helen hopped up on stage, and everything started to smell like pizza bagels. Then, instead of Helen, there was just a big purple fog on stage. I went to find the cause of the pizza bagel smell, but before long, everyone was screaming that Betty was dead."

"Wow. Okay, tell me this: do you know Betty?"

"Know Betty? No, man, she's dead."

"Fantastic. Please just send in whoever is next."

Linda was the next to sit in the vacant chair.

"Boys, please make this quick if you can. I'm critically ill, and I need to get home as soon as possible. The priest gave me last rites tonight, I'm afraid to say."

"I'm sorry to hear that. I can have a nurse come by, or we can take your statement from the hospital if that would make things easier on you."

"No thanks, I'll be fine. But make it quick. If I sit for too long, my pancreas just starts screaming bloody murder."

"Jesus, I'm so sorry. Cancer?"

"I don't know, do you think it could be? Dear God! I better check my symptoms on WebMD." Linda grabbed her phone from her purse and began typing in a panic.

"First, please just answer a few questions. Describe what happened tonight and your relationship with the deceased."

"This was just another mixer. Elaine plans all these fancy events, and tonight she had a wine and cheese tasting, never mind that dairy makes me gassy and wine gives me hives. So, I just sat here hungry, neglected, dying all the while. I did share a bit of Cheez Whiz with Brenda, though, just to be polite. And then I heard someone screaming that Betty was dead in the bathroom. Can you imagine? Betty died before me, even though my doctor swears up and down that I have a nearly fatal case of hypochondria. I might be the first person to die of it! I'm going to be in medical textbooks," Linda said with a satisfied smile on her face.

"Very impressive, ma'am. What about Betty? How well did you know her?"

"Oh, Betty. I didn't know her that well. We slow danced a few times at events at the clubhouse, but she was pretty quiet. She loved to garden. Sometimes she coughed right into her hands and then would touch the door handles, so no, I wouldn't say we were close at all. I made sure to keep my distance because of my health."

"Thanks so much for your time, Linda."

The night stretched into the early morning hours. A few times, the officers had to make their way back into the main clubhouse area and break up a striptease, much to their surprise. Problem was, the women had to stay put, so they sat around the buffet table and did their best to polish off the wine. Finally, after what felt like many hours of investigation, they called Judith to the room.

"Hi, Officers, my name is Judith Fletcher. Just tell me what you need to know. I'm the newest one here, so I'm not sure what help I'll be. I'll do what I can, but I just moved in today—er, yesterday, I guess. Normally I'd be pretty nervous about this place with the murder and all, but I'm not. Can you beat that?"

"Alright, Judith. We're not calling it a murder yet. We're just investigating, so tell us what happened tonight, and then we'll let you get some sleep."

Judith gave them the most comprehensive chain of events from the evening, yet it proved relatively useless for the two cops in terms of figuring out what happened to the dead woman.

"Thank you for your time. We'll keep in touch. Since Betty didn't mention any known health conditions to her friends and was relatively young, we're going to proceed as if this was a suspicious death. Without any obvious injury to the body, we have to consider the possibility of an overdose, a suicide, or even a potentially criminal manner of death. Tell everyone to stay in Florida and keep their cell phones handy."

Chapter Five

Who Let the Dogs Out?

I don't want to hear the word murder again for the rest of my life. And ladies, I certainly don't want to hear it this weekend. All I want to hear is you all telling me about someone looking hot and half-dressed," Brenda announced as the ladies packed the last of their luggage into the large van they had rented. She was excited about the trip. For her, Fantasy Fest was better than Christmas. And hot women were the gifts under the tree.

"I realize the murderer could very well be in this van, but I don't care. We aren't going to speak of the murder, think about the murder, or even acknowledge the murder until we are back from Fantasy Fest. Are we in agreement?" Brenda demanded.

"The theme of Fantasy Fest this year is crime and punishment. I have a feeling murder and death will be a bit hard to escape, even on vacation," Elaine said.

"Murder is never far from my mind, and I doubt the next few days will be any different," Wheezer rasped, climbing into the back and putting on headphones.

"I can't believe Wheezer came. She's their main suspect, you know," Brenda whispered to Judith. "Just be careful. Don't be caught alone with her."

"I didn't think they had any suspects just yet. I'll be careful, though." The last of the women piled into the vehicle, with Elaine in the driver's seat and Judith by her side. Judith had not planned on taking a vacation before she was fully settled into her new home. All Brenda had to do was mention that Elaine was attending, and there was no way Judith could say no.

Jo piped up from the back. "I know we're not supposed to talk about it, but did the cops say anything about me? Did they ask you questions about me? They made me empty my pockets, and I had my lock picking set! I mean, I didn't do anything. Wheezer is the one who opened the door in the first place."

"Wheezer's their main suspect, you know," Brenda offered again, her eyes dilated and her tone rising. This gossip was just too good not to share. "They'd have arrested her by now but there's no evidence yet, probably because she's a criminal mastermind!"

"Shh! She can hear you!" Linda was sitting right next to Wheezer, whose eyes were closed as she relaxed on her neck pillow.

"No, she can't. She has headphones on, you nervous Nelly," Brenda said.

"She couldn't hear you anyway, she's half deaf," said Elaine.

"They are at least considering the possibility it was foul play," Judith said, timidly.

"I knew it!" Brenda said. "Now, no more talk of Betty. I want to hear exactly how crazy everyone is planning on getting this weekend. I think we should all get our tatas painted. Last year, I got mine painted like a pair of dogs. Do y'all remember? My nips were their noses. It was the cutest little design, and the adorable gal who painted them kept singing 'who let the dogs out!' We should do a big theme painting together for the Masquerade March."

"I'm in if everyone else is," Linda said. "I've never done it before, and I might as well do something daring before I die, which could be any day now, you know."

Brenda rolled her eyes. "Judith? Elaine? Are y'all too chicken?"

"I'll do it if we can find a decent artist. I don't want something sloppy or in poor taste," Elaine said.

"I'm in!" Judith exclaimed, surprising herself.

"Alright, now let's think of a good idea. Crime and punishment, hmm..." Brenda said, rummaging through her sewing bag until she found her latest project, cross stitching 'Eat a Bag of Dicks' to send to the current asshole in the governor's office. "I'm thinking we focus on the punishment side. Maybe we could all dress up like submissives and flip a coin for who gets to go as the dominatrix."

"Of course that's what *you* would suggest, Brenda. Sex is all you think about. You're going to regret it once you're as sick as I am," Linda said.

"Nah, let's go for the crime angle. What if we dress up as bank robbers with gun holsters painted on our hips?" Jo asked.

"Now, I just want to be clear. I am not going to be fully naked," Brenda said, to the other women's surprise. "Topless is as far as I care to go. And Linda, I'll have you know that I think about plenty of non-sexual things. It's not my fault that once I moved into a den of lesbians, I became a bit wanton. I spent my whole life being a virtuous Southern woman. In fact, I was a virgin when I moved in."

"Really, Brenda. You were a virgin when you were fifty? Aren't you divorced?" Jo asked.

"Yes, I sure was a virgin. I mean, at least partially. We got divorced because I was too pure to have sex. That's a fact. I simply wouldn't debase myself."

"As I recall, you were married to a man," Linda said.

"Exactly. What on earth kind of lesbian would I be if I had given in and had sex with him? Especially him. Other men, maybe, but my husband was no looker. I didn't even come out until we divorced. Probably no one in this car will believe me, but it's the truth. I have fifty years of pent-up sexual energy, and you better believe I'm going to spend the rest of my life using it to the fullest."

Elaine turned on some quiet radio music in the background.

"More power to you," Jo said, her fingers running through her short hair. "I came out when I was fifteen, and my parents kicked me right out of the house, of course. But I got by doing odd jobs, and I became sort of a Jo-of-all-trades. The funny thing is, I'm not divorced. I lived with my partner for twenty-five years, but marriage wasn't legal when we got together. She left me, and I can't even say I'm divorced. After twenty-five years, I deserve to call it something with a little more gravitas than a break-up."

Cynthia chimed in. "I told my family that I'm gay, and they didn't care. I'm just lucky, I guess. Boy, were they surprised when I married a man. As a matter of fact, so was I!"

Judith spoke up next.

"I never came out to my family, but I never really dated, either. I just focused on my career. My friends always knew, but my family wouldn't have tolerated it. So, there's this part of me that they never really knew about. That's one of the reasons I moved out here. I don't want to have to live a lie anymore."

"Here, here!" shouted Linda. Wheezer didn't even blink. "I never came out to my family, either. I had a thirty-year 'roommate' who came with me to all my family events: weddings, bar mitzvahs, Passover. They never said a thing about it. They aren't the brightest bulbs, though. My gal died some years back of breast cancer. It crushed me. But look at me now, living my dream even as I approach my own deathbed."

"What about you, Elaine?" Brenda asked.

"I don't want to talk about it."

"Come on, the rest of us did. It's not like it's easy for anyone, especially women of our generation," Brenda prodded.

"Alright, fine. I told my mom, who made me promise never to tell another living soul. When they found me kissing another girl, they sent me off to a camp so some minister could 'fix' me. I thought it would be horrible, but honestly, I made a lot of friends. After-hours, the place was practically a nonstop orgy. I came home, said the camp worked, and lied to my parents all through college so they would continue to pay for my education. After graduation, I never spoke to them again."

"That's just terrible, Elaine. I'm so sorry," Brenda said. "We're your family now. Let's talk about something happier. We're going on vacation, for Christ's sake. Where were we? Oh, yes, taking our tops off and getting painted. That's much more pleasant."

"We could go as famous female serial killers," Judith suggested.

"Yes! That's a great idea. I'm claiming Countess Elizabeth Bathory, who they say bathed in the blood of virgins. I'll get to be half-naked and elegant at the same time," Elaine chimed in.

"Aileen Wuornos, the man-killer!" Jo shouted.

"Bonnie Parker is who I want," Linda said. "You know, of Bonnie and Clyde? I'm not sure she killed anyone, but probably."

No one had noticed Wheezer removing her headphones. "Why are we yelling about criminals?"

"We're deciding on our group costume—we're getting our titties painted for the festivities. We're going as famous female murderers. Maybe you can just go as yourself," Brenda said.

"For God's sake, Brenda, I didn't kill Betty. In all likelihood, Betty wasn't murdered. And I'm certainly not going topless."

"Why? Do you have something to hide there in your bosom?" Brenda asked as she gestured toward Wheezer's chest.

Wheezer sighed a long sigh. "I don't even know why I came on this silly trip. I knew you all would spoil it with your idiotic ideas. Fine, I'll get my saggy old boobs painted. But only if everyone agrees to stop treating me like a criminal."

"Yes! This is going to be so much fun. I can't wait to see all those ladies half-naked and, with any luck, drunk. If I play my cards right, I may not have to sleep in my room the whole weekend!" Brenda said.

After nearly eight hours of driving, the women finally arrived in Key West. The island city was already hopping with traffic and tourists prepping for the festivities ahead. Cops were blocking off streets, and outdoor vendors were setting out their wares along Duvall Street.

Brenda always thought it felt a bit like a gay Mardi Gras. By her own estimation, she deserved some debauchery more than most. She finished up her dick-themed cross stitching and put it in her bag. She was already thinking about her next project—a pornographic wall hanging for the clubhouse.

The weather in Key West was hot, and many people were strolling the streets in minimal clothing. Brenda smiled to herself. She was getting older, but she knew she was still desirable. She had no problem securing dates, something that she was proud of as a sixty-five-year-old. Her animal magnetism was only getting stronger, she thought. Just a quick shower, and she would be off to find her next hookup. *I don't even want to know her name,* thought Brenda. *I just want to show up, show her a good time, and then I'll be on to the next one.*

When they parked, Brenda looked around to take in the place. They were staying in a classically styled hotel with a lovely pool and tennis courts. They never bothered splurging on a luxury resort because there was just too damned much to do. They didn't spend much time sleeping.

Once they had checked in, Brenda began her well-honed getting-ready-for-sex routine. She started with a nice, warm shower, lathering up with the fragrant coconut body wash provided by the hotel. She trimmed her nails, of course, and then painted them fire engine red. She threw on a breezy, low-cut dress and took a bit more time to do her makeup and hair, making sure every pore and strand looked just so. She applied her favorite perfume, right between her breasts. She added a tiny dab below her belly button, for good measure.

Next, she needed to pack in case she lucked out and didn't come back to her hotel room that night. Some lube, gloves, and a little bullet vibrator went into a velvet pouch that she tucked in her purse. She placed a strap-on and belt into the main compartment. Then she added her reading glasses, a travel-size toothbrush and toothpaste, and her phone charger. She just barely had enough room for her wallet.

Before leaving her room to meet her friends for dinner, she took a long glance in the full-body mirror. "I'm ready for anything and fuckable as ever," Brenda affirmed to herself as she locked the door on her way to meet up with her friends.

Chapter Six

Brenda's Got Game

B renda was ready before anyone else was, of course. She had to knock on each woman's door and goose them a bit to get ready. They only had a couple of days at Fantasy Fest, and the clock was ticking.

"Elaine, how much more primping can you possibly do?" Brenda said as Judith sat on the bed in Elaine's hotel room, flipping through the channels and waiting patiently.

"I don't consider basic hygiene to be primping, Brenda. I had to shower, exfoliate and moisturize, apply a face mask, set my hair, paint my toenails, re-moisturize, select coordinating jewelry, and—"

"Why? By the time you're done, it will be time for bed. Hurry up, Elaine! I'll go round up the rest of our crew. But by God, you'd better be ready to go when I return. There are ladies out there that are in dire need of what I can provide. If I turn up too late, they may have the misfortune of going home with someone else. Someone else, Elaine!" Brenda spun on her heels and knocked on the next door down.

"Cynthia? You ready yet?" Cynthia opened the door, and a whoosh of grass-tinged air met Brenda's nose. "For Christ's sake, you haven't even gotten in the shower yet, have you? Get in the shower, Cynthia."

"Oh, a shower! Good idea, Brenda. Do you want a lollipop?"

"No, I do not, Cynthia. What I want is for your ass to be ready for dinner. Can you remember that?" Cynthia rolled her eyes and shut the door, so Brenda headed for the next hotel room down the hall.

"Linda, time for dinner!" Brenda's knocks were getting louder and more frantic with each passing minute. "Linda! Goddammit, answer me!"

Linda came to the door in her nightgown, rubbing her temples, and holding a box of tissues. "Oh my goodness, Brenda. I'm having a flare-up of some sort, maybe rheumatism. I think someone must have been eating snacks with gluten on the way up. Can you believe that? Risking my health when I'm already suffering so?"

Brenda took a deep breath and swallowed the scream building in her throat. "Linda, the only thing we had in the car was fruit. You are not even allergic to gluten. And you better get your suffering ass into something respectable and be ready for dinner in five minutes, or you will wish one of these diseases had killed you. I'll make sure of it!" Brenda slammed the door and stomped down to Jo's room, where the door was already ajar.

"Jo? Trusty, reliable, old Jo? You're ready for dinner, aren't you?"

"Well, yes, of course. I hope this outfit is good enough. But I just got my tools out. You know, the air conditioner was making a funny sound, and I took it apart and found something really strange inside. Brenda, you're not going to believe it—"

"I don't believe it now, Jo. We were supposed to be out, wandering around, meeting women, and eating our effing dinner thirty minutes ago. But not one of you is ready. I'm going to go check on Wheezer. Surely she's ready, unless she has another dead body to clean up."

Brenda stormed out and knocked on Wheezer's door. "I'm not going," Wheezer shouted back through the closed door. Of course you're not, Brenda muttered to herself as she returned to Judith and Elaine.

"Y'all finally ready? Because no one else is. I'm about to dine by myself and leave you guys here to get takeout. I'm not squandering my first night of vacation because you're all too selfish to come cruising with me."

"Calm down, Brenda. We're ready. And just look at Elaine! She's worth every moment, isn't she?" Judith said sheepishly as Elaine did a twirl in her far-too-fancy dress, at least by Brenda's estimation. Brenda grabbed both their hands, careful not to lose any progress as they made their way back down the hall. Cynthia poked her head out of her hotel room door. She had clearly forgone the shower, but at least she was dressed.

"Yuck, Cynthia, you smell like the hallway of my freshman dorm," Brenda said, ushering the women further down the hall.

"If so, then your dorm-mates were smoking Red Headed Stranger, which is très magnifique," Cynthia said as she blew a chef's kiss with her fingers toward the ceiling. "They must have been terribly clear-headed and motivated."

"Not so much, Cynthia. They were potheads. And if I miss meeting my red-headed stranger because you were smoking your Red Headed Stranger, I will never forgive you," Brenda said. Cynthia stuck her tongue out at Brenda and knocked on Jo's door. Brenda knocked on Linda's. The women finally appeared, seemingly prepared.

"Finally! Are y'all ready to meet some women?" Her crew of friends seemed to roll their eyes in unison, already annoyed with Brenda's unrelenting zeal for getting laid at Fantasy Fest. Then Brenda stopped suddenly. "Oh, my God! Girls! I left my business cards in my hotel room. I have to stop and get them."

"What do you need business cards for?"

"They're more like 'getting-down-to-business cards,' you could say. They have my phone number, address, email, and social media listed, you know, in case anyone I meet wants to stay in touch or spend another night with me," Brenda said with a sly smile.

"For fuck's sake, it's the twenty-first century, Brenda! Just put your phone number in her phone. The elevator's here!" Cynthia said.

"No, it's literally my calling card. I even pass them out to the women who don't go home with me right away. It's why I'm such a successful sexual networker. Go on without me. I'll be in the next elevator down, promise," Brenda exclaimed, running back to her room.

Two minutes later, cards in hand and a fresh lipstick smear on her lips, Brenda pushed the elevator button once again, ready for her absolute favorite event of the year. She took a deep breath, and when the elevator doors opened, Brenda's jaw dropped. Before her stood a gorgeous woman wearing a white tennis outfit and a sweaty pink glow. She heard herself swallow and walked forward casually. "Hi," she said, regaining composure.

"Hi," said the woman standing before her. "Do I know you?"

"Not yet," Brenda said with her most charming smile.

"Strange. You look familiar," the woman said.

"I get that a lot. I'm heading to dinner with some friends. Want to join me?"

"I would, but I'm heading back to my hotel room to shower off.

I just played a match at the courts next door. How about you join me instead?" This was precisely why Brenda loved athletes. Always straightforward, only playing games on the court.

"You read my mind," Brenda said. They got off on the second floor, and Brenda followed her to her room. "Are you going to Fantasy Fest?"

"Yes, isn't everyone? I just had to squeeze in a little physical activity first."

"I'm delighted to squeeze in a little activity before dinner, too. I'm Brenda, by the way."

"You can call me Annette because I'm always standing in the middle of a tennis court," she said, chuckling. Then she added, "but really, my name is Nancy." Nancy took Brenda's hand and guided her directly into the bathroom. Brenda set her bag of essentials on the counter and watched as Nancy removed her tennis visor and freed her straight brown hair from its ponytail. Damp strands stuck to her face and neck as Nancy untied her pristine white tennis shoes. Her tennis outfit crumpled in a pile on the floor, and she bent over to turn on the shower water. Nancy had no shame at all, Brenda noted enviously, but that was probably due to her picture-perfect body.

"Wow, I really should have taken up tennis," Brenda said to Nancy, visibly admiring her form.

"Come on in, the water's fine!" Nancy shouted above the roar of shower water. The lighting wasn't ideal in Brenda's opinion, but she wasn't about to let her vanity come between her and a good time. Brenda slipped out of her dress and didn't even notice her perfectly applied makeup sliding off in the humidity, her perfume rinsing gently away.

"Nancy, can I wash your hair?" Brenda asked, shampoo bottle already in hand. When Nancy nodded, Brenda poured a lavish amount into her palms and created a silky lather. She rubbed Nancy's warm temples and massaged her scalp. Nancy was just short enough that Brenda's arms didn't fall asleep, which was a plus. Over the years, Brenda had seduced many a woman with her sensual shampoo technique. The final signature touch was a thorough rinse and tender grazing of the jawline and earlobes.

Brenda took another moment to admire Nancy. She was tan in the areas left subject to the sun by her tennis outfit, and the pale skin underneath almost looked like the white tennis outfit she had worn before. She was muscular and just barely curvy. Breathtaking, Brenda thought.

Nancy offered the hotel's small bottle of body wash to Brenda. "Now, all you have left is the rest of me," she said with a wink. In no time, both women were covered in coconut-scented suds.

Feeling Nancy's slippery skin under the suds, Brenda kissed her new friend's lips and then went to work rinsing the suds from Nancy with the detachable shower head, paying particular attention to her thighs, breasts, and abdomen. Slowly, she rinsed between her legs, then let her hands roam exactly where they wanted to go. It didn't take long until Nancy's breathing became deep and rhythmic. Nancy's orgasm came quickly, and Brenda took a mental snapshot of it, so she could recall it later when she was alone. Nancy's face was a mixture of relaxation and focus, her lips just slightly parted, and her eyes closed. It was beautiful, and Brenda wanted to remember it so she could fantasize about it when she touched herself.

Afterward, Brenda toweled off and said, "I appreciate how forthcoming you are. Most women want me to wine and dine them."

"Not me," said Nancy. "You've probably heard the joke that to a tennis player, love means nothing. But, in my case, it's mostly true. I'm not looking for anything serious. I'm just looking for a good time. And Brenda, you didn't let me down. Want to order some room service? Your friends have probably forgotten you by now."

"Good idea," Brenda said, glancing at her phone for the first time in an hour. Forty-six missed texts. Elaine was probably irate. Cynthia had probably not even noticed that Brenda was absent. Linda and Jo wouldn't mind, though. They were the most forgiving of the bunch. Of course, she couldn't say for sure about Judith. Judith was still an unknown.

As Nancy ordered a bottle of medium-dry Riesling and a couple of club sandwiches, Brenda shot off a quick text to her friend group so they wouldn't wonder if she was as dead as Betty.

Sorry I didn't show. Met a gal. I'll meet you later on tonight. Don't let Linda drink too much. You know when she gets dizzy, she always thinks she has brain cancer.

A knock at the door meant the orders had arrived with surprising alacrity. Nancy had already turned on some nature show in the background to cover up the awkward silence.

"Come on in," Nancy said, and Brenda jumped up.

"Let me buy," Brenda said before she had seen the hotel employee delivering the food. As Brenda turned toward her, she decided her karma must be clean as a whistle. The employee holding the tray of food was a cute woman with long blond hair wearing a dapper hotel uniform. She seemed to be in her mid-fifties.

"I just need to scan your hotel key," said the employee.

"Of course." Brenda went to the bathroom to retrieve it. At the door, when Nancy was out of view, she handed the employee both her hotel room key and her calling card. She winked and mouthed, "call me." She had forgotten that she closely resembled a drowned rat, not having fixed herself up after the shower.

The mischievous smile that spread across the employee's lips gave Brenda some hope that the room service woman wasn't straight. As soon as Brenda relaxed on the bed with a bite of sandwich, her phone rang.

"Hey, we just met a few minutes ago. I go off duty in five minutes. Want to meet me in your room? I saw your key so I know where it is."

"Yes, of course, I can be there in five minutes." Brenda said, her mouth still full. "Nancy, that was a friend of mine. I have to run. I'm so sorry." Brenda took a giant bite out of the club sandwich—she knew she would need the endurance—and left a calling card on the desk in Nancy's hotel room. "Maybe we'll run into each other again."

As Brenda gathered her things and left, it occurred to her just how unkempt she looked. Oh well, she thought. I'm still a hot commodity.

The room service woman was right outside her hotel room door, as promised, still wearing the uniform and a knowing smile.

"I'm so glad you called," Brenda said.

"Was that your girlfriend?" the woman asked her.

"No, no girlfriend. Just a friend." Brenda slid the key into the slot until it blinked green. "What's your name?"

"Samantha—yours?"

"Brenda." As she awkwardly extended her hand forward, the lawyer in her took over. "Nice to meet you."

"I assume you're here for Fantasy Fest," Samantha said.

"I'm just here to meet women," Brenda said as she leaned in to kiss Samantha.

"Actually, I was hoping we could talk a little bit first," Samantha said, ducking her advance.

"Oh, sure." Brenda kicked off her heels, took a deep breath, and sat down on the bed. If she had known this was going to be a long-simmering seduction, she would have brought the rest of her sandwich to help pass the time. "What do you want to talk about?"

"What do you do for a living? Where are you from?"

"Lawyer. Charleston, originally, though now I'm a full-blooded Floridian. And yourself?" She wasn't trying to be unfriendly, but she had gotten into a rhythm with Nancy and wanted to keep up the pace. Nancy had not returned the favor in the shower, and Brenda felt the blood congesting her lady parts.

"Room Service. Key West."

"Oh, right," said Brenda.

"Well, that's enough talk. I just didn't want to come off as too fast," said Samantha.

Those were the magic words Brenda wanted to hear. Brenda quickly peeled Samantha out of her shirt. She was curvy and gorgeous, and her touch of deviousness turned Brenda on even more. Brenda kissed her deeply. Kissing someone, especially a stranger, always had the effect of making Brenda introspective. She thought, for a moment, of the questions her friends would ask when she met up with them for breakfast tomorrow. Why, for instance, did she need to sleep around so much?

"You are a great kisser," Samantha said, quietly moaning into Brenda's mouth. Despite the delicious make-out session, Brenda's mind continued to whirl with questions. Brenda had a no-tolerance policy for slut shaming, and she didn't care a lick what her friends thought about her after-hours activities. But she did hate that her friends thought she was sliding into a cliché; that pent-up Brenda was turning her golden years into a nonstop orgy.

Brenda deftly undid the buttons on Samantha's uniform and slid her pants down around her ankles. She was beautiful. As Brenda slowly kissed her way down Samantha's tummy, her thoughts tangled. She saw her suitcase sitting next to the hotel room desk and remembered packing up her belongings when she and Gary finally got a divorce. She found a diary her mother gave her right before she got engaged. Brenda's first entry was something she had written on her wedding day, many years ago:

Today, my life starts. I'm Mrs. Gary Howard! I can't wait to fill up this book with my many adventures.

Sadly, that was the only entry.

Brenda made some drastic life changes after she left Gary. She was proud of her many conquests and adventures, and how she built her post-divorce life into something tantalizing and enviable. She lived every subsequent moment on her own terms. But sometimes she wondered: how much casual sex would be enough to pay down the debt of a mostly sexless and invisible life? It wasn't as if she didn't enjoy the casual sex—she enjoyed it immensely. But she thought of her therapist, in the back of her mind, asking whether she was afraid to be as disappointed by a woman as much as she was by Gary. It had been many years, but she still felt crushed by the empty allegiance of being a wife to someone who never knew her at all. What a waste, she thought.

One of Brenda's favorite parts about sex was the way it sometimes turned off her brain and allowed her complete enjoyment, free of self-judgment. Kissing made her feel thoughtful, but down and dirty sex did not. Brenda felt her concerns melting away as she moved down and got into a rhythm of kissing, licking, and moving that maximized the deepness of Samantha's breath. It was hypnotic. And it was over a bit too quickly for Brenda's liking. She wanted to spend the remainder of the evening pleasuring Samantha. But after a short while, Samantha exhaled deeply and said, "your turn."

"Oh, thanks, Samantha, but it's late. I had a great time," Brenda knew this part by heart, and she said it without thinking as she looked for her shoe. She loved touching other women, but sometimes, it was hard to let them reciprocate. "I'd love to see you again sometime if fate allows it."

"You can skip the pleasantries if you're just going to kick me out," Samantha said, sounding annoyed. Brenda knew this part by heart, too. She knew that comforting Samantha could be misread as intent to continue, to force some kind of relationship to begin. So, she just left the uncomfortable sentence in the air.

As soon as Samantha had gone out the door with puppy dog eyes and a parting glance, Brenda picked up her phone and read a text from Jo:

I hope you found someone to take home. Really missed you tonight! My door is always open if you didn't luck out ;)

Brenda smiled as she read the message. Jo always understood her and never required anything of Brenda other than to be herself. Brenda knocked on Jo's door and saw her adorable sleepy eyes and her hands peeking out of an over-sized bathrobe holding a bag of microwave popcorn, and knew she'd made the right decision. She found herself cuddled up next to Jo, too tired for anything more, and grateful for the people who were her inner circle now. They knew her and loved her, and it meant a great deal more to her than a marriage ever had.

Chapter Seven

The Secret Pearl Detective Club

The Secret Pearl women were rushing to get ready for Betty's funeral, trying to assemble a carpool where the most punctual didn't kill the least punctual first.

"Who's riding with me?" Judith called out, gesturing to a mostly empty Jeep. Cynthia yelled, "I'll take shotgun!" But the look on Elaine's face showed her that seat was already reserved. "Or a backseat. I just don't want to drive right now, if you get my drift."

"We can smell your drift from the driveway, Cynthia," Elaine shot back. Brenda piled in the Jeep, too, and the others rode with Linda.

"Now, I just can't bear to hear another word of what I missed during Fantasy Fest." Brenda lamented from the backseat. "I mean, I wasn't exactly missing it. But it still feels like salt in the wound to hear about all your fun."

"You didn't even leave the hotel," Cynthia chuckled, leaning her forehead on the cool window.

"I tried, believe me, I tried. There were just so many beautiful, enthusiastic women right there on-site. I cannot stomach the fact that I missed the wet t-shirt contest and didn't have a single slice of key lime pie. You know that's my favorite post-coital treat!" Brenda pouted. "But you should see my journal. I haven't even had time yet to capture each moment of my vacation." They pulled up into the church parking lot and noted that Wheezer had driven herself.

"Of course she didn't carpool. It's not enough that she killed Betty, she wants to murder the environment, too," Cynthia remarked before the women went inside.

Mercifully, the funeral was short. There was some singing of hymns, a brief slideshow of photos of Betty when she was younger, and a short reading by one of her sisters, someone they'd never met.

"What a dish!" Brenda whispered to the women when pictures of a younger Betty on a beach vacation were displayed. She was in a sexy string bikini that left almost nothing to the imagination. "I've seen thicker dental floss," Brenda added, gesturing to Betty's protruding nipples.

"For God's sake, we're at a funeral, Brenda. Show some fucking respect," Cynthia said, before passing down some brownie bites to the ladies. "The frosting has a touch of Alaskan Thunder Fuck in it. You're going to love it."

The rest of the funeral passed in a haze for Cynthia. Her grandkids were coming over later that day, and she was so excited to see them she could think of nothing else. Some of the women cried during the slideshow, but Cynthia noticed Wheezer sitting stone-faced, idly scrolling on her phone throughout most of the ceremony. Apparently, some of the other women had noticed, too, because, over refreshments, it was all anyone could talk about.

"I hope Betty's family was watching Wheezer. She has some nerve coming to Betty's funeral. But being rude on top of it? It's too much. It's just too much," Brenda said, after she stopped Linda from accosting a second worker to ask if the buffet contained any traces of shellfish.

"I'm not sure why you're all so certain she killed Betty. There's no evidence!" Judith countered, trying to imbue some reason into the gossip circle that was underway.

"Okay, exhibit A: Wheezer was the only one who knew Betty *very* well. Exhibit B: Wheezer has always been a bitch. Exhibit C: did anyone see Wheezer drinking the wine? I didn't. Wheezer loves wine. She could have poisoned her," Cynthia exclaimed.

"I hate to ruin your Nancy Drew moment, Cynthia, but that's not technically evidence. It would never stand in court," Brenda noted, always happy to put her law degree to use. "If being a bitch was evidence, then Wheezer would already be in jail. And just because you didn't see her drinking wine doesn't mean it didn't happen. You were so stoned I bet you can't list one coherent detail from that night."

"Look at this. Her birth date on the memorial program is quite a bit earlier than I thought. Did she lie about her age?" Cynthia interrupted Elaine's cross examination and waved the front of the program. "It says she was born in nineteen-forty-four. Is that right? I thought she was about sixty-five."

"Yeah, that doesn't seem right. Maybe we should ask Wheezer," Elaine said. "Hey, Wheezer! Why don't you clear up a few things about your relationship with Betty? We're all so very curious."

"I spent a long weekend with you at Fantasy Fest. If I didn't change your mind then, what would be different now?" Wheezer replied, picking up a wafer cookie at the refreshment table. "You idiots can't tell the difference between a gruff old lady and a murderer. I can't help you with that. What do you want me to do? Cry? She's dead, and nothing is going to bring her back. If you need your little detective club to distract yourselves from the fact that we are all aging, and sooner or later, we will end up just like Betty, then go for it."

Cynthia burst out giggling. "You guys, we *should* have a detective club. Just like Scooby Doo! There are so many mysteries to solve at the Secret Pearl. First on the list is 'The Case of Why Wheezer's Such a Goddamn Bitch All the Time.'"

"Well, if you could solve a mystery just by getting high, I'm sure you'd already have cracked the case, Cynthia," Wheezer said.

"Cut it out, you two. You're acting like children. The whole point is for us to show up for Betty today and pay our respects," Elaine said as she wandered over to the casket. She put her hand on the top of it and looked at the date on the memorial program again. "Whatever deal you struck with the devil to look so good, Betty, please haunt me and let me know so I can strike the same one."

"No one is taking this seriously," Linda said, dabbing a tissue at her eyes. "Betty deserved better than to die on a toilet with her pants down, alone, at a party. Elaine, is touching the casket such a good idea? We still haven't ruled out the chance she had something contagious." Linda pulled hand sanitizer out of her purse and offered it around, but was met with a chorus of rolled eyes.

"How the hell would she have touched the outside of the casket, Linda?"

"Well, my respects have been paid in full, and my grandchildren are probably almost here. Judith, do you want to come and meet my grandchildren? They're more fun than a dime bag." Cynthia was beaming.

"Sure, my schedule is wide open," Judith said, and Elaine nodded that she would tag along, too. Linda overheard, and Jo agreed to come, though they hadn't been specifically invited. Brenda gestured that she would also be there in no time. That was the trouble with retirement—often, no one had conflicting plans when it was convenient. Everyone assumed they were invited to every event.

When the ladies arrived at Cynthia's home, Cynthia's daughter Christine was already in the yard, unloading her two girls from her wagon-style minivan.

"I'll be back before dinner. No pot stories, mom. I mean it. None. Not even one. Got it?"

"Yes, Christine, don't get yourself all out of joint, ha. You know you can count on me." Christine raised an eyebrow and gave Cynthia an uncertain look.

"Thanks, mom. Ryan and I are just going to look at some summer properties this afternoon. It would be nice to have a place so close to you. Who knows, maybe we'll turn into snowbirds." Christine got back inside the minivan, put it into reverse, and rolled down the windows again. "No pot stories!"

Christine's girls had matching backpacks and long, gleaming black hair. One was in sixth grade and the other in eighth. They were Cynthia's pride and joy, although she didn't always understand them. They were vastly different from Cynthia, and yet they got along so well. "Ivy, Ava, meet the Secret Pearl gang. Secret Pearl gang, these are the youngsters who hold the keys to my heart." Cynthia kissed the tops of their heads. "I'm going to go make us some munchies."

Cynthia disappeared in the kitchen and reappeared shortly with grapes, cheese, crackers, and juice boxes. "What would you like to do today, girls?"

"Math, grandma. Can we do math together? Or we could help you sort through your storage shed. It seriously could use a good cleaning, unless you cleaned it since our last visit. You said you were going to. Did you?"

"Well, no. Not yet. I've been busy." At this, the girls rolled their eyes. Grandma Cynthia was never that busy. "Math, really? What about finger-painting or watching *Finding Nemo*? That movie is so funny. The fish forgets things just like I do." Cynthia laughed and removed a lollipop from the pocket of her shirt. Thinking better of it, she replaced it and patted the pocket closed.

"Grandma, you know we're too old for that. I'm going to be in high school next year. And actually, what I'd really like is to ask you some questions. Big questions. Like why you're so happy all the time. Our parents aren't happy all the time. They're always talking about real estate tax breaks or bickering over home décor and parental duties. But you're always so relaxed and happy. And when I'm old, I want to be like that, too. I don't want to be a Debbie Downer like mom."

Cynthia pulled out her phone, which was croaking with frog noises. It was a text from her daughter.

No pot stories, mom!

"What is she, psychic?" Cynthia thought for a moment. "That is a big question, girls. I'm not sure I'm the right person to ask. But these women who are with us, well, they're the smartest people I know. And they're all incredibly happy, too. I'm sure between the lot of us, we can pull together some good advice."

Judith and Elaine exchanged glances.

"Well, I never had kids, and I'm not much on giving advice. I give good advice to animals, though, because I'm an animal doctor," said Judith after a long pause.

"You can say veterinarian," Ava said. "We're not babies."

"My best is advice is just to know what you like. If you like math, don't let anyone—even your grandma—tell you it's a waste of time," Elaine said.

"The best advice I ever got was never to check your symptoms on WebMD," Linda said. "But I've just never been able to take that advice myself."

"Love as many people as you can before settling down," Brenda said. "I didn't do that, and I often regret it."

"Don't marry a man," Cynthia finally said to her grandchildren. Elaine gave Cynthia a stern look and an elbow to the ribs. "What? It's the best advice I have. I've dated men, and I've dated women. When you date men, you can't expect an orgasm, but he will expect dinner on the table every night. It's the opposite with women."

"Now your daughter's going to think you're trying to turn them into lesbians," Linda whispered.

"I can no more turn them into lesbians than I could turn them into croaking toads. I'm just telling them how to be happy."

Chapter Eight

Oh My Eyes

E laine sat at her desk, staring at a blank calendar. She'd been having a hard time planning more events after what happened to Betty, but realized the girls needed a morale boost. Even though they'd returned from Fantasy Fest not long ago, spirits were flagging and tempers were flaring. Events were the way Elaine brought people together. But she just wasn't sure that bringing people together was the best idea, at least before the murder suspect had been apprehended or the medical examiner had at least determined the cause of death.

Judith, though, had been dutifully contacting the cops, trying to get confirmation on the cause of death, but there was a backlog of cases at their local police station. As Elaine's mind turned to Judith, her lips transformed themselves automatically into a smile. Judith had only been half joking when she wondered if a serial killer was on the loose, murdering left and right and keeping the police too busy to solve Betty's case. Yet at the funeral, Betty's family seemed happy to accept that she had likely died of natural causes. But those who found her on the toilet were skeptical. *It would be nice just to get some resolution,* thought Elaine.

Elaine decided then and there that she would pay Judith a visit. Once her thoughts turned to Judith, it was difficult to think of anything else. Planning a new event was not in the cards for her today, and she could use some company. She and Judith had practically been attached at the hip since Judith's move to the Secret Pearl, a new experience for Elaine. Usually, Elaine took her time getting to know people, keeping them at a proper distance until she'd thoroughly vetted them. But something about Judith caught her off guard, disarmed her, and she found herself telling Judith things no one else knew. She felt like family—not the sort of family that Elaine grew up with, but the idea of family she grew up hearing about, the kind that made any place feel like home and any day feel like a holiday.

Also atypical for Elaine was the fact that she didn't apply and reapply makeup before seeing Judith; she had once even worn the same outfit two days in a row. Since Judith always made her feel attractive, her high maintenance routine was devolving into a moderate maintenance routine. Elaine had never felt more desirable than when Judith was looking at her. So, abandoning her usual need to change or freshen up, Elaine headed across the well-worn path to Judith's place.

Elaine saw Judith sitting at her desk with her reading glasses on, shuffling through papers as Hannibird Lecter perched on her shoulder. Judith's eyes were bright and her hair was wild, unusual enough that it registered an uptick in Elaine's pace across the driveway. Judith spotted Elaine through the window and urgently waved her in.

"Elaine, you are never going to believe this. I just got off the phone with the police," Judith said, heading into the kitchen to pour them both some iced tea. Elaine was happy that the need for greetings and pleasantries had been entirely forgotten and they had reached the stage of their relationship where they were in a permanent, days-long conversation. "They were asking if Betty had recently had plastic surgery. Apparently, she had a long history of plastic surgery, and they're trying to determine whether she may have died from the complications of some botched operation or medical malfeasance. Oh, and please don't mind this crazy fur family. Clawdia, Cat Benatar, and Pussy Galore have been plotting something together, I'm sure of it. The cats were circling Elaine with suspicion, or perhaps just hoping to seduce her for treats.

"What the fuck? What the fuck?" Hannibird Lecter piped up from Judith's shoulder. He always had a way of inserting himself into the conversation. Judith's cats were less conversational but no less observant. Elaine had a certain intuition about pets and their social dynamics. Right off the bat, she'd been able to tell that Clawdia was friendly, Cat Benatar was the dominant one, and Pussy Galore was just beautiful, though a bit impulsive. The cats seemed to get along with Hannibird for the most part, as much as predator and prey ever can. Elaine had loved animals from the day she was born, and meeting Judith's little family had endeared her to Judith all the more. Elaine sat with Judith at the kitchen counter and Clawdia immediately made herself at home in Elaine's lap.

"You have got to be kidding," Elaine said, getting back to the current crisis as she ignored the parrot and sipped her tea. "That explains why she looked so young. I still can't believe she was as old as she was. It's just not fair."

"If she had as many operations as the police think, I'm wondering if she had some hidden wealth we didn't know about, too. Maybe she was killed for her money. I didn't even think to ask anyone at the funeral who stood to benefit financially from her death."

"Yes, I think asking that at the funeral would have caused quite a stir, Judith," Elaine noted dryly.

"I know. I would have never actually done it. But the suspense is killing me, and the police aren't making any progress. There has to be some logic to this. I'll sleep better when we know whether this was a murder or not. Won't you?"

Judith's smile reached her eyes, and they had a touch of mischief inside. Whatever tomfoolery Judith was up to, Elaine wanted to be involved—intimately.

"I mean, I could have performed the autopsy by now," Judith said. "I can't believe how long this is taking. I wonder if they're investigating something bigger or if this is part of a giant scandal. It might explain why Betty's family was so eager to believe that she died of natural causes. Natural causes don't just strike suddenly while you're on the toilet, do they? Natural causes creep up slowly, and you die eventually, in bed, surrounded by family. At least, that's how I always pictured it. I still remember my mom talking about how my Grandma Violet hovered between life and death for many hours, if not days. Though I do remember how Mom got up to go to the bathroom, and grandma died before she got back." Elaine wasn't following her closely as she was more focused on Judith's sweet, clean smell. Judith wore a light brown cardigan with the top button undone and blue fitted slacks. It was a boring outfit, to be sure, but Elaine couldn't stop thinking about undoing more of those buttons.

"You're probably right. I've never seen anyone die before. But the look on her face just didn't seem natural to me." Elaine felt a wave of bravery well up inside and decided to change the topic. "Judith, I have to ask something. Am I alone in thinking that this—" Elaine gestured wildly between them "—is something good? I don't mean to be vague. It's just that you make me feel like a schoolgirl again. How can I tell if we're dating, when you're already one of my closest friends and we spend every waking minute together? It's on my mind, and I don't want to pretend that it's not. I'm too old for that."

Judith didn't rush a long sip of her tea, and the silence was long enough to give someone less confident than Elaine a small heart attack.

"Of course we're dating. Or, I suppose I should say we're about to date. I've known that sex was a foregone conclusion for us since the moment I saw you. I was just waiting for you to catch up," Judith said with a playful smile. "Sometimes, you're a bit slow on the uptake."

Elaine let out a deep breath she hadn't realized she was holding in and returned Judith's smile. She felt her cheeks burning and her heart quickening. It had been such a long time since she'd had this pleasant rush of adrenaline, the kind that only came right before sex with someone for the first time.

But Judith wasn't someone new. Sure, sex would transform their relationship into something new, yet Judith felt incredibly familiar to Elaine. They had only known each other a little while, but Elaine already had trouble remembering what her pre-Judith life was like, or why on earth it was meaningful. But the familiarity made Elaine no less nervous. Here she was at the start of something big and serious, and she felt terrified of screwing it up.

"Are you going to sit there blushing, or are you going to kiss me?" Judith asked, circling her finger around the top of her glass of iced tea. When Hannibird screeched "Kiss me! Kiss me," she remembered he was still on her shoulder and she carried him gently back to his cage. Clawdia took the hint as well and sprang from Elaine's lap.

"I do want to kiss you. I'm just afraid of rushing things. Everything is already so perfect. I don't know how to change it and I don't want to ruin it."

Judith, it seemed, knew how to change it. She leaned in and kissed Elaine softly on her lips, and despite the familiarity, everything felt new for the both of them. Judith's hands felt new on Elaine's back after she'd gently removed Elaine's sundress. They felt like they belonged there, and they already had precise command over exactly how Elaine liked to be touched.

Elaine helped Judith undress and was silenced by the sight of her friend naked. Judith looked comfortable without any clothes on, and her skin was pale, blushing in spots, and velvety soft under Elaine's touch. Their breasts were not in the same place as they were in their twenties, but the magic was that neither of them cared. No one worried about showing only their most flattering angle or hiding their wrinkles or belly rolls. There were only hands and mouths and wetness and a distinct feeling of being truly seen by the other.

It's true what they say about sex being a drug, thought Elaine. *I just didn't realize the drug was like Advil.* They were on the floor, incredibly, for hours without a pain or cramp. Or perhaps there were pains and cramps, but the pleasure flooded out any other sensation. The only sounds—save a few parrot curses and the occasional cat meow—were their gasping and sighs. The only smell was their now-mixed breaths and the natural fragrance of their slightly damp bodies.

Elaine's mouth moved naturally down until she came to Judith's deepest ache. She wet her fingers and slowly dipped them inside Judith. Her slick ridges and valleys felt like a discovery to Elaine's tentative fingertips. Her lips and tongue, usually so self-sure, now felt concerned that they were in the wrong spot, using a strange rhythm. She became hyper-aware of each motion, and Judith's breath indicated that she appreciated the extra attention. In minutes, Judith came effortlessly, and her face eased from joyful tension to utter relaxation.

Judith returned the favor, and underneath her touch, Elaine felt incapable of any further apprehension. Her muscles relaxed with each passing graze from Judith's hands, her nipples stiffened, and she climaxed without willing herself to do so. Everything happened so naturally that all prior sex felt forced, uncomfortable, and even strange. As they lay on the floor together, Judith's head resting on Elaine's stomach, they sighed in unison. Their moment of rhapsody was interrupted by Hannibird, who was watching them from his cage.

"I've seen enough. That's enough!"

"We should have started doing that as soon as we met," Judith said.

"I wouldn't change a thing about what happened between us, actually," said Elaine.

Elaine knew that the ease with which they both came bordered on a miracle. Post-menopausal sex was amazing, but it had very little in common with the sex she was used to from her twenties and thirties.

Sex took a bit of trying and exploring, which she knew they would get to eventually. Having an orgasm without much effort was like seeing a double rainbow—and as Elaine had gotten older, she swore she would never take sex for granted again.

A few minutes later, reality barged in and ruined their post-coital love bubble. Elaine's arm was numb from Judith resting against it, and Judith's back gave her some trouble when she tried getting up into a seated position.

"I'll get the Advil," said Judith, when she was at last able to stand.

"Next time, let's buck tradition and do it in a bed," said Elaine.

"My eyes! Oh, my eyes!" Hannibird screamed.

Chapter Nine

Wheezer's Recollections

There was a photograph from Betty's funeral that Wheezer couldn't get out of her head. While it had been taken only a few years ago, it symbolized something that had haunted her for a long time.

And now that she was thinking about it, she wasn't sure why she went to the funeral at all. Everyone, even the people who were supposed to be her friends, had already pegged her as Betty's killer—before the police had even decided it *was* a murder. Sure, Wheezer was grumpy, but she hadn't had any idea that those closest to her thought she could kill someone in cold blood.

Wheezer had never been capable of real harm of any kind, save the crass comments and occasional insults. She tried not to be insulting, but she was unfailingly honest. It was important to her to be honest. So, if someone looked like crap, she told them. If someone had perky tits, she told them. Not having a filter anymore was her favorite part of growing older.

Wheezer had a filter once, and it was burdensome. Throughout childhood, she wore herself out trying to be an A+ student, a loving daughter, and an accomplished pianist. All so her parents would love her. Deep down, she knew her sexuality would eventually disappoint them, and she hoped to make it up to them in advance. So, she baked bread early on Saturdays (her mother bragged that her brother Martin made delicious triple layer cakes). She got a job delivering papers as soon as she was old enough (while Martin had a fast-track internship with a renowned engineering firm), and was the Class President and Valedictorian (Martin didn't need a scholarship since the military paid for his college). No matter what she accomplished, her parents never seemed impressed with her.

She sent her folks money when she became a colorectal surgeon (she had often joked that her career allowed her to recognize an asshole when she saw one). Lots of money, actually, and she received nothing in return. Sometimes she would double-check her bank statements to make sure they cashed the checks. And when her parents got old, they moved in with Wheezer. They didn't move in with Martin, whom they fawned over, because he was in the Navy. They moved in with trusty old Wheezer, who took care of them day and night, up until the very end. She kept her secret from them, too, because she never seemed to earn enough credit with them to pay the toll that coming out as a lesbian would take on their fragile relationship. It wasn't until after they died that it occurred to her they'd never really had a relationship at all.

As her mom was dying, her brain addled with dementia, Wheezer held her hand and asked the question she had always avoided: why don't you like me? Through cracked lips, her mom pulled her closer and whispered, "because you are tedious."

Wheezer had expected to hear a story about a difficult pregnancy or labor, or perhaps that her parents had hoped to have another boy. But boring? That was a slap in the face. The worst part was realizing it was true, at least a little true. She spent her whole life trying to be perfect, and perfect people tend to be boring. She never considered whether or not being a surgeon would be fun or fulfilling; she just knew she could develop the skill set, the tolerance for the pressure. In the end, she stayed closeted because of people who didn't like her even when she was pretending to be something she wasn't.

Now Wheezer was never something she wasn't. She didn't put on a sunshiny face for anyone. She said what she meant, and she never walked it back. It was freeing, even if it hadn't brought her any happiness. *I'm not boring anymore, mom,* Wheezer thought. *But I am a first class bitch.*

That picture of Betty really stuck in Wheezer's craw. The picture showed Betty smiling, carefree on the beach, in the arms of some beautiful woman in a two-piece swimsuit. Wheezer knew which summer it had been because it was before Betty's last facelift—

that much was evident from the picture. Her cheeks were rosy and glistening, something that only happened to Betty's face when she was in lust—or just after an orgasm.

Wheezer knew that look well. There was only one summer that Wheezer could remember being genuinely happy, and it happened about five years ago. She was as much curmudgeon then as she was now, but somehow the universe found a way to drive a burning hot wedge into the ice of her cold, black heart. And to Wheezer, her heart wasn't that icy, it just had a protective layer that kept out the riff-raff; most of the world was riff-raff.

Wheezer had not dated much, just the occasional college episode of "experimentation," as the other women called it. And she certainly hadn't fallen in love. The very idea of settling down before the age of fifty seemed to her reckless, unwise, and premature. And yet, the moment she met Betty, she felt very reckless and unwise indeed.

Wheezer remembered it as if it were yesterday. The day Wheezer had moved into the Secret Pearl, Betty had showed up on her doorstep, all perky, with some baked goods. Betty had on the prettiest apron; bright yellow covered with white daisies. Her hair hung in curls about her face.

"Welcome to Secret Pearl. Try one," Betty said, handing Wheezer a muffin with a grin.

"It's good, but I like fruit muffins better than chocolate chip," Wheezer said, unsmiling.

"I'll take that as a thank-you," Betty said with a laugh. Betty had a way of smoothing over all of Wheezer's rough edges and making the world seem amusing rather than dreary.

"You can take it however you want," Wheezer said. "I didn't move here to make friends."

"Then let's not be friends!" Betty said cheerfully.

"You've got yourself a deal," Wheezer said, smiling for the first time that day.

"Well, I should warn you. I take all the newcomers here line dancing. But since we're not going to be friends, I guess you can skip it."

"I like line dancing, I'll have you know. And I'm not half bad at it."

"Great! Then I'll pick you up at seven," Betty said as she deposited the assortment of treats in one of Wheezer's bowls she found rummaging freely in her cupboard. Somehow Wheezer had been asked on a date and accepted, all without meaning to. That's how it went with Betty. Everything happened naturally, even when Wheezer was trying to be a pain.

Betty Black loved line dancing and baking, and Wheezer loved Betty. Just a few weeks in, this was evident. But Betty was young at heart. Even on the surface she looked quite young, and she didn't seem the slightest bit interested in settling down. This was something Wheezer understood inherently. Wheezer had never imagined anyone would want to settle down with her, but she hadn't imagined she would fall in love, either. Betty was funny and fun-loving, beautiful, and smart. If anything, Wheezer was shocked they had gotten together in the first place. But it was as if Wheezer's sadistic realism buoyed Betty to reality, and for a short while, it worked.

Eventually, it all became too much for Betty. Wheezer was insecure, paranoid, and suspicious every time they weren't in the same room together. At some point, Betty's attention seemed to be elsewhere, no matter what they did together. So Wheezer started acting crazy: showing up unannounced, going through Betty's text messages, and questioning her whenever she didn't answer her phone. Wheezer knew the breakup was coming and was powerless to do anything about it. By the time Betty got around to ending her relationship with Wheezer, it had already crumbled into dust.

Seeing a picture from the period of time they'd been together brought back all these feelings for Wheezer. And the rancor of confirming that she had, in fact, found someone else so quickly after they broke up—or perhaps even during their relationship—really ruffled Wheezer's feathers. Maybe Wheezer's jealousy wasn't so crazy after all. Her negative view of the world often proved to be prescient, and she was devastated that she was correct; the small victory of being right felt rather pyrrhic. Knowing that Wheezer hadn't ruined the relationship all on her own didn't come as much of a relief. *That's what I get for being vulnerable,* Wheezer thought. *Never again.*

When it came to Betty, jealousy had made Wheezer crazy at times. Once, she even put her fist through the wall, which was probably the last straw for Betty. The jealousy made her feel crazy even now, as she looked down and saw both her hands chalk white, balled into fists. Of course the one person she had ever loved had been cheating on her. Why had she ever imagined this wouldn't be the case? Maybe Betty had deserved to die on a toilet for all to see. Wheezer shook her head, frowning, knowing it wasn't true.

Chapter Ten

Brenda Has a Side Dish

I *f I hear one more word about murder, I'll go absolutely stark raving mad,* Brenda thought to herself. The Secret Pearl girls had been buzzing about, from one residence to the next, asking questions about Betty and worrying about the murderer who was ostensibly on the loose.

"Did you hear that sound in the middle of the night? There was a big crash!" Jo said, after stopping over for some coffee at Brenda's place. "I thought the murderer was here to take me. But I think I could have stopped them if I tried. I used to have a black belt in karate, you know." Jo threw a couple of chops into the air as a demonstration.

"That doesn't surprise me in the least," Brenda said. "But I'm not sure what good karate would do against poison. That's the way Betty died. Everybody thinks so."

Jo had stopped by each morning to make sure Brenda had made it home from her frequent extra-curricular activities. It was cute, in a way, but Brenda was about ready to confess to the damn crime if it meant everyone would stop talking about it. Even Jo was preoccupied with Betty's death now.

Desperate times called for desperate measures, so Brenda called upon he-who-shall-not-be-named. And he-who-shall-not-be-named, as Brenda referred to him, was not God as many people thought. Brenda was far too practical to be bamboozled by religion. He-who-shall-not-be-named actually had a name, and that name was Gregory.

But she didn't like to mention him around the Secret Pearl ladies, because they might accuse her of treason.

After all, it was a little bit treasonous to sneak out of a dyke-filled community for a tryst with a man. But that's precisely what Brenda needed. She found that men her age were fairly good at having sex without the need for any further relationship; you just had to properly vet them first. But only Gregory was up to the task of reciprocating in bed. She met him several summers ago, when he did some landscaping around Secret Pearl. He was sweet and handsome, if not the sharpest tool in the drawer she'd ever seduced. Better yet, he was reliable. Any time she texted, he was ready for a get-together, always at his place because she couldn't bear to have anyone see a man leaving her house in the morning.

If the girls ever asked where she went, she said she was going to Lydia's house. It was a lie, to be sure, but Lydia did exist. Lydia was a stunning lady that Brenda met one year at Fantasy Fest. To Brenda's chagrin, Lydia had rejected her flirtation. So, Brenda decided to make the best of the situation and pretend like they were involved anyway. Greg was even listed in Brenda's phone as Lydia, just to provide extra insurance that no one would ever discover her little secret. Brenda decided it was time to make the call.

"Hey, Greg. I need to see you as soon as possible. Everyone is driving me nuts! There was a murder here—not sure if you've read about it in the news, but it's all anyone can think about. I need you to make me think about something besides murder."

"Understood. Want to come over for dinner tomorrow? I'll grill steaks."

"That sounds terrific. I'll bring wine. Bye, Lydia. Er, Greg."

When Brenda arrived the next night, she was surprised to find an older woman sitting on his front porch. Brenda walked up and extended a hand to her.

"Hello, I'm Brenda. Is Greg at home?"

"Yes, he told me you were coming. I'm his mother, Martha. He's out back, making us some steaks."

Brenda's eyes widened momentarily, and then she gave her best fake smile and let herself through the gate to the backyard.

"Hi, Greg. Did you invite your mother over for a threesome?"

"No, no. I just thought it was about time you met her," Greg said, grinding some pepper over the ribeyes. He gave Brenda a side hug and kissed her on the cheek.

"Why in the world would I need to meet your mother, Greg? We're fuck buddies. I'm practically a toaster oven-worthy lesbian. Did you forget that?"

"Uh, I'm not sure what that means, but can't fuck buddies have milestones, too? We've been doing this for well over a year now," Greg said as he gestured to the air between them. "Come on, don't be mad, you're going to love her."

"I will probably love her a lot more than I love you, Greg. I can't believe you blindsided me like this."

"One man's blindside is another's romantic surprise," Greg said. "Go grab three glasses and pour us some of that lovely red you brought."

Brenda went inside, shaking her head, and made her way toward the bar. She found the appropriate glasses and the wine opener and set about opening up the wine. Greg's mom was so quiet that Brenda didn't even hear her enter the room.

"You really know your way around the place," Martha said with a wink. Brenda smiled graciously but was cussing up a storm on the inside. What kind of nonsense was this? This kind of bullshit made her wish she were one-hundred percent lesbian. Men could never read the room. The time it must save to never need their services.

In the backyard, Greg had set the table for three with candles lit and rose petals sprinkled on top. Greg's mom put a pretty, pink box in the center of the table. God, Brenda hated pink—and roses. Brenda liked leather and lingerie.

"That's for later," his mom said, tapping the box with a twinkle in her eye. Underneath the table, Brenda texted Jo: *Mayday!* In a matter of seconds, Jo's phone call vibrated Brenda's phone. Jo always came in handy in situations like these.

"Oh, hi, Jo! You've caught me at a bad time. I'm eating dinner and can't talk right now. What's that? An emergency, you say? Yes, I'll be on my way in just—" Greg's mom took the phone from Brenda, and Brenda found herself too shocked to object.

"Sorry to interrupt, but this is a big, special night for Greg and Brenda. Any chance you can handle this emergency on your own?"

Brenda heard Jo sputter and fail to come up with a compelling lie. Martha hung up the phone. Brenda was too shocked to move.

"I'm just relieved it was a woman on the line. I'd hate to think my dear Greg was getting cheated on," Martha said, and Brenda nearly choked on her wine.

When Greg came over with the steaks, Brenda chimed in. "Jo is having an emergency, so I really can't stay long."

"You have to eat at some point. Better do it now before you deal with Jo's 'emergency.'" Greg's air quotes made it clear that no one believed Jo was having an emergency. *Fuck*, thought Brenda. Greg placed a perfectly grilled hunk of meat on each plate and went into the kitchen to fetch the sides.

"I taught my boy how to cook. He's quite a catch," Martha said, sipping some wine.

"Yes, someday, someone will be lucky to have him," Brenda said, refusing to make eye contact with the optimistic old lady.

"I think that day might be sooner than you expect," Greg's mom said.

So this is where Greg gets his tone-deafness from, thought Brenda. Greg returned with a pan of collard greens and a drool-worthy basket of Southern-style biscuits nestled in his elbow. He served everyone before sitting down, always the gentleman.

"Happy anniversary, Brenda," he said without a trace of irony in his eye.

"Anniversary of what?" Brenda said through gritted teeth.

"We've been, well, getting to know each other over the past eighteen months. And I thought it was about time to celebrate." Greg nodded to his mom. She nudged the neatly wrapped pink box toward Brenda.

"Go on, open it. It's an anniversary present," Greg's mom said.

Brenda took the package and felt obliged to open it, giving Greg the stink-eye the whole time. Inside were two gorgeous ruby earrings.

"My God, these are beautiful!" Brenda said, forgetting the awkward situation for a moment.

"They were my mom's, and now they're yours," Martha said, eyes glistening.

"I can't possibly accept these. It's just that—Greg and I, we're not really serious, yet," Brenda said, hoping to avoid crushing his mother with the information.

"Sometimes, you just need a little push to get from casual to serious," Martha said. "Come on, put them on. They're just your color." Brenda obliged and then tucked into her steak, eager to fast-track the evening's purgatory. *If Jo were a real friend, she'd be on her way over here to come and save me,* Brenda thought until she realized that Jo didn't know who Greg was or why she was with Greg instead of Lydia. The dinner went on for what felt like a week. The only topic of discussion was why Brenda and Greg were such a great couple, and Brenda really had nothing to contribute. She distracted herself by trying to remember Greg's last name. It definitely started with an S. Or maybe that was Lydia's last name.

When Greg's mom had finally taken her last bite, Brenda stood up abruptly and offered to clear the dishes. She brought as much as she could carry inside, set the plates down by the sink, and kept walking straight for the front door.

"You leaving so quickly?" Greg said from behind her.

"Of course I am! What kind of a sick joke is this? We're not dating, Greg. We've never even been to a restaurant together. Why does your mom think we're destined for marriage?"

"She just wants to see me happy, settled down."

"You're sixty years old, Greg. You're as settled as you're going to get."

"Are you really going to leave before you get what you came for?" He gazed at her slyly, trouble in his eyes.

"Are you really going to do me while I'm wearing your grandmother's ruby earrings? Should I ask if I can borrow your mom's diaphragm, too?"

"That won't be possible, Brenda. My mom hasn't needed a diaphragm in quite a long time."

"Yes, Greg. I'm leaving. Or should I stay here and tell your mom we're going to retire to your bedroom for some intercourse? We could tell her that having sex is the only thing we do together because that's the truth, Greg."

"Her TV shows are on now. She won't even notice. Come on. I'll make it up to you," he said. Brenda followed him upstairs begrudgingly, figuring that an orgasm would at least make the night seem less like a total loss. They quickly undressed and had nearly silent sex, so as not to be overheard. It was over in a blink, and before long, they heard a knock at the bedroom door.

"Come in, ma," Greg said, not giving Brenda quite enough time to cover up with a sheet. Nipples akimbo, Brenda straightened her hair and blushed as Greg's mom entered the room.

"I thought I heard some rustling around," Greg's mom said to both of them. "I brought you some warm towels to clean up." Greg's mom turned to leave, but something caught her attention. "Wearing nothing but earrings, huh? That's what Greg's dad liked, too," she said with a devious grin.

And this confirmed what Brenda had always postulated: she did love occasional dick, but it was rarely worth all the drama she had to endure to get it.

Chapter Eleven

Potion Emotion

T hough Elaine always wanted credit for being the official Secret Pearl event organizer, she had failed to plan any events as of late, spending most of her time at Judith's, investigating Betty's death, no doubt. So, Cynthia took up the reins and invited the ladies over for a little get-together. She was proud of herself for putting together something thoughtful, and she even remembered to put it on her calendar. She was certain this rendezvous would be one to remember.

"Ladies, this event is the culmination of years of effort on my part. Since my teenaged years, I have been experimenting, trying to combine the right ingredients together to make the perfect aphrodisiac. And I'm happy to tell you that I've done it, I've finally done it!" Cynthia had rehearsed this speech briefly before her friends arrived, and in her mind, it was met with applause. But the ladies who now sat before her reacted only with skeptical looks. Cynthia was, for some reason, dressed a bit like a fortune teller, with a purple scarf wrapped around her salt and pepper hair, and a flowing white dress that billowed around her.

"Ten bucks says it's just weed," Wheezer said, and for once, everyone nodded in agreement.

"Tell us what misfortune lies in our future, oh Cynthia the clairvoyant," Brenda said, shaking her head.

"It's not just weed, Wheezer! Come on you guys. I worked really hard on this."

"She forgot her crystal ball, I guess," Brenda whispered to the ladies.

"Alright, one more snide comment, and you don't get to try it! I can just use it myself."

"Don't be like that, Cynthia. We're excited to try it," Jo said, as Brenda rolled her eyes.

"This is an ancient remedy, a potion for boosting your libidos in unimaginable ways." Cynthia held up a purple jar, and upon closer inspection, saw that the jar was covered in a thick layer of dust. She wiped part of it on her clothes, leaving a big brown smear across her white dress. "The chemical properties give you both physiological and psychological effects. The psychological effects will increase your desire like never before. The physiological effects will help you relax and increase blood flow, which will make you feel like a horny teenager all over again. Good for both body and mind, this potion will awaken you to your most primal of senses." With a flourish, Cynthia poured a small amount of the tincture in the purple jar into a pan.

"Did you memorize that little speech?" Wheezer asked, and Cynthia did her best to ignore her. She had memorized her speeches, of course, because when she didn't have them down word-for-word, she often forgot what she wanted to say entirely. She heated the pan over the stove and poured a small amount of milk on top of the tincture.

"Milk? What exactly are you making? You know milk makes me gassy, and that's the opposite of sexy," Linda piped up.

"This is almond milk, Linda. I don't drink cow's milk either. It's disgusting and unnatural."

"Almond milk is disgusting and unnatural if you ask me. How the hell does someone milk a nut? We lesbians have no business drinking nut milk, if you ask me," Wheezer said to no one in particular.

"That reminds me: I almost forgot to tell you all my big announcement. Not quite as big as this groundbreaking potion I've come up with, but big nonetheless." Cynthia took a big breath and turned away from the stove to address everyone. "Guys, I've decided I'm a vegan!"

"Oh, for fuck's sake. This party is worse than the one where Betty was murdered. I'm out of here," Wheezer said, grabbing her large handbag and making her way to the door.

"Did you hear that? She admitted Betty was murdered!" Brenda whispered.

"Will your veganism last longer than your commitment to keto?" Linda added with a giggle.

"Oh, shut your pie holes, ladies. From now on, I'm only interested in eating natural food that was grown in the ground. No more animal products in this house, only plants." After a few more moments of stirring, she got out some white porcelain mugs and set them across the countertop. She poured a brown liquid into each mug.

"What exactly are we drinking?" Judith asked.

"It will taste just like hot chocolate, ladies. Chocolate, milk, a bit of sugar, and my special secret blend of sexy stimulants. Enjoy!" Cynthia passed out the mugs and downed hers in one gulp. It took a moment for anyone else to venture a taste.

"Nothing more refreshing than drinking hot chocolate on a boiling Florida evening, am I right? I'm just going to do it," Brenda said with a sigh. She took a small sip and grimaced, then smiled. "Hey, it's not half bad! A little earthy, but drinkable." She drank the rest quickly, and the other women followed suit. *Not bad* seemed to be the consensus, but it was a little short of the high praise Cynthia had expected.

"So, how quickly will we feel it? I'm getting a little nervous, drinking mystery juice with all my health problems," Linda said, scratching her fingernails underneath her collar.

"Should take just about twenty minutes to an hour. It depends a little bit on how much you've eaten today," Cynthia said, licking the last drops out of her warm pot. The elixir was delicious, she thought, and anyone who disagreed with her was welcome to go straight to hell.

"So, are y'all going to just sit here until we feel incredibly horny, and then make excuses to go home to your vibrators? Or are you game for something a bit more interesting?" Brenda asked, wiggling her eyebrows at Jo.

"I'm up for anything," Cynthia said. "If you're not, just wait an hour, and perhaps you'll change your mind. Anyone want to join me for some reruns of *Gentleman Jack?*"

"You know it," said Jo, grabbing a beer out of Cynthia's refrigerator to wash out the chocolate-y taste and making her way into the den.

"That's a great idea, Cynthia. We can play a drinking game. Wait, no, better yet, a stripping game! Every time the music swells to a crescendo or they cut to a shot of lush Victorian countryside, we lose a piece of clothing. Got it?" Brenda said.

"Or any time one of the Anns wears something you wish you could pull off," Jo added.

"In that case, everyone is going to be naked, fast. I just hope the aphrodisiac kicks in first. Could we get some better lighting, Cynthia? Got any candles?" Linda asked. "My bra and underwear don't match. I need lighting on my side."

"I have incense and a lava lamp, how about that?" Cynthia said, heading into her bedroom to dig out some ambiance supplies. Linda's comment caused Cynthia to shut the door briefly and change out of her boring undies into something a little sexier, and in no time, she was armed with patchouli, her incense burner, lava lamp, and some lube.

When she returned to the room, it was quiet. The ladies were either enraptured by the show or the calm of her potion had taken ahold of them. Jo sat on the couch, touching her suspenders, wondering if they counted as an article. She put her hat back on, too, conceivably wanting to be the last person naked. Brenda sat next to her, dressed in business casual slacks and a dress shirt, eyes scanning the screen for any plot points that would necessitate the removal of more clothing. Next to Brenda was all that was left of Wheezer—a butt imprint on the couch. She wished, for a moment, that Wheezer had decided to stay; an odd number of guests was always the cornerstone of an effective orgy. But the girls might have more fun without Wheezer and the constant cloud of doom that followed her wherever she went. Judith and Elaine sat so near each other that the loveseat seemed to be able to fit three people instead of just two. Linda sat on the faux pleather easy chair, which she had thoroughly wiped down with an antibacterial wipe before inhabiting. Cynthia smiled at her friends. Retirement was so much more fun than she had ever expected.

"Anne Lister is my spirit animal," Jo said, eyes trained on the screen.

"Anne Lister is everyone's spirit animal," Linda said.

"Nope, not me. I'm one-hundred percent Ann Walker," said Brenda.

"But Ann Walker didn't sleep with everyone she met. You're no more Ann Walker than I am," Jo said with a smile.

Cynthia plugged in her lava lamp and lit the incense. "How am I going to know if your potion worked, Cynthia? Or if I need another round?" Jo asked.

"Oh, you'll know. Look at Linda—it hit her hard."

Linda was slumped back on the couch, a broad smile across her face, rubbing lotion all over her arms and hands. Brenda was sitting very still, watching the television show closely. And Elaine was laughing in every scene of *Gentleman Jack*—especially the parts that weren't funny. Yes, Cynthia was sure that the potion was working.

"It's time," Cynthia said. "Verdant landscape shot! Everyone loses a piece of clothing. Your watch doesn't count, Linda."

"Look at that top hat and cane," Jo said, taking off her socks. "I would kill for an outfit like that. Not literally, of course. My apologies to Betty, may she rest in peace."

"My body feels like it's buzzing," Elaine said, taking off her blouse. "I can't believe your potion actually works, Cynthia! No offense, of course. Judith, you don't get to skip out on our game of strip-*Jack* just because you didn't finish your potion."

"Oh, right." Judith had been busy watching Elaine undress. "I did finish—it just took me a while." Judith showed her empty mug to Elaine as proof.

"I'm shocked," Elaine said with a giggle.

"It's a bit unlike me, I know," Judith said, as she shook off her shoes.

The rest of the group realized that they had become invisible to the pair. It was as if Judith and Elaine were enclosed by a glass pane that separated them from the group and from their own sense of modesty. The sound of chaste Victorian accents was soon overcome by zippers, slacks crumpling, and good-natured laughter. The spell that Cynthia had cast was at full tilt. She fought the urge to talk more about the ingredients, how long she had spent perfecting it, and why it was so effective, but instead decided to give in to its powers. Cynthia undid her scarf and, in one fluid motion, swept her dress up over her head and onto the small mountain of clothes.

Time seemed to slow down a bit, and Betty's death was the last thing on anyone's minds. Cynthia glanced across the living room in time to see Brenda's thighs part on her sofa, and Jo leaped off the couch to kneel in front of her. Nearly everyone was already paired off.

Linda had removed her checkered dress shirt and shorts; all that was left to see was her curvy build, olive skin, and Rachel Maddow-esque glasses. Cynthia raised an eyebrow to Linda, and Linda nodded and patted a spot on her lap as reserved for Cynthia. Linda had short, silvery hair and her fear of death had always overshadowed the chaotic, masculine energy that Cynthia now observed. Though nothing romantic or sexual had ever transpired between Linda and Cynthia before, the potion had them both feeling open-minded and ready to try something—or someone—new.

"I like to do women with my fingers," Linda said. "That okay with you?"

Cynthia wondered, for a moment, if this was because Linda was scared of sexually transmitted diseases, or if it was truly her preference. But the dominance in Linda's voice silenced any further questions in Cynthia's mind.

"My hands are very clean, I just sanitized them, in fact," Linda said, offering her fingernails up for inspection.

"Linda, I have never once wondered whether your hands were clean," Cynthia said as she shimmied out of her red, lacy underwear. She leaned back to give Linda a better angle, and Brenda leaned over from in front of the couch to squeeze Cynthia's hand. Brenda and Jo switched places, with Jo sitting on the couch and Brenda now kneeling between Jo's legs.

"Great party," Brenda said, out of breath from whatever magic Jo had just performed between her legs.

Cynthia had not been fingered in a while; too long, she thought. She poured a few drops of her favorite CBD lube onto Linda's hand, relaxing as Linda slowly rubbed the cool liquid in circles around her own secret pearl, eventually spreading it inside her, too. Linda worked slowly and methodically. Cynthia's breath slowed as she relaxed into the pace of Linda's fingers and the haze of the party. Whether she was like that for minutes or hours was hard to tell, but she enjoyed every second of it.

From what seemed far away, she heard Judith's breath rush to a crescendo, and then a bit later, Jo's did the same. Ever since menopause, Cynthia's orgasms came a bit fewer and further between. It wasn't that she lacked desire, though that had waned ever so slightly, too, but something had shifted inside her. Perhaps she enjoyed the buildup more, and she focused less on the fireworks. But whatever it was, whether the potion had served as a distraction or the naked bodies of her friends were diverting her attention, today was not a day she would finish.

Cynthia rose slowly and nakedly in front of Linda, slipping gently away from her probing fingers.

"Do you want me to stop?"

"I'm not done with you yet," Cynthia said. "Someday, I want a rain check when we're alone, and I want you to do exactly what you were doing today. I just have too many thoughts rattling around in my brain right now."

"Deal," said Linda, as she took out a wipe from her pocket to clean off her pruny fingers. The women lay in couples, sleepily and quietly across Cynthia's living room. Elaine was playing with Judith's hair, and Jo was whispering something into Brenda's ear.

"Alright, I demand to know what was in that potion," Elaine said. "I've never behaved like that in my entire life. You said it wasn't weed, so what the hell was it?"

"No, I said it wasn't just weed. It was a Bettie Page tincture, mixed with dark chocolate, Nutella, and milk. I infused the Bettie Page into some cocoa butter. And believe me, it took a while to get the perfect timing and temperature. You've got to cook it slowly, or you'll destroy the THC—"

"What the eff is Bettie Page?" Brenda asked.

"It's a strain of marijuana, silly," Cynthia said. "It's known for the body euphoria and clarity it provides. It's creativity minus any dry eye; you really can't top it for sex. I've tried probably eighty different strains, and this is the best by far. I mean, what's a better aphrodisiac than Bettie Page?"

Chapter Twelve

Helen's Secret History

Helen Davis stood in her modern and sophisticated kitchen, thrilled that the Florida temperature had finally relented from scorching to merely sweltering, and she could make her famous fried coconut shrimp. Her air conditioning worked perfectly, but sometimes the heat from her late morning gardening lingered inside her body and made the thought of standing over a pot of hot oil inconceivable. She walked to her small wine cellar and selected bottles of white Sancerre, Vinho Verde, and Riesling.

I'm going to come up with the best pairing for coconut shrimp if it kills me, she thought. Uncharacteristically, she always had trouble when deciding what to pair with her signature dish. Should the wine reflect the pepperiness of the spices? The fruitiness of the dipping sauce? Or the creamy sweetness of the shrimp and coconut? She had narrowed it down, but tonight she would declare one wine the victor.

Helen heard a knock at her door and saw Judith standing outside. "Well, hello, Judith! Come on in."

"Sorry to drop by unannounced, Helen, but I received a letter I believe was meant for you. I'm guessing it's because you're at thirty-two-seventy and I'm at thirty-seven-twenty. Delivering the mail must be so mind-numbing, it's no wonder the numbers start to blur together!" Judith said with a friendly smile, turning to leave.

"Thanks, neighbor! Do you want to come in? I've got shrimp ready to fry and three bottles of wine I'm going to open that I can't finish by myself."

"You said the magic word: wine!" Judith said as she entered the house.

"Fantastic. We'll have a taste test. You'd think pairing wine with coconut shrimp would be an easy task for a sommelier, but you'd be surprised. You can do a red, but it depends on how high the iron content of the soil is, where the grapes are grown. Too much iron and your mouth is going to taste like anchovy paste after a bite of shrimp. So, we're going to try some of my favorite whites." Helen turned on the stove and gracefully uncorked the Vinho Verde. "It's a nice surprise to have some company! I don't typically find the time or energy to attend the Secret Pearl's social events, but I do love visitors. If you weren't here, I'd be spitting away all this fancy wine into my bucket. Cheers!"

"I'm usually a red gal, myself, but I'm excited to try a pairing by a professional sommelier." Judith slipped her phone out of her pants pocket and shot off a quick text. "Sorry, I just want to let Elaine know that I won't be home for dinner tonight."

"Ooh, do I smell a romance?"

"Yes, actually. We recently started dating. And even a brand new relationship couldn't tear me away from the allure of a home-cooked meal and wine pairing with a sommelier. I should have dropped by sooner, Helen," Judith said. "So, where are you from?"

Helen filled a bucket with ice, placed the two remaining bottles inside, and brought it over to the dining room table. Her décor was minimalist, black and silver, and more modern than most of the other resident's manufactured homes. Helen wore dress slacks, a dress shirt, tie, and blazer when she wasn't gardening, which accounted for why she found her kitchen so unbearably hot during Florida summer days.

"Originally? Americus, Georgia."

"Never heard of it," Judith said, visibly enjoying the wine.

"You're not missing much, but that's where I was born and raised. My parents worked at the local grocery store there. I got a scholarship and went to college in New York, studied the culinary arts, and eventually ended up in France as a sommelier. A master sommelier, in fact. But since my ancestors were actually slaves, you can understand why I'm uncomfortable with that term." Helen smiled and adjusted the cuff of her blazer. "I worked in and around restaurants for years and decided to retire somewhere a bit warmer than France or New York so I could be closer to my folks. How did you end up here?"

"About the same as you. I was a veterinarian in Minnesota, so I've served my time in snow country. I wanted a new start, somewhere I could be myself. And here I am! So far, the Secret Pearl feels like a perfect fit. Uh-oh, if I don't slow down, I'm not going to have any left by the time the shrimp are ready to eat." Judith pushed the glass of white away and smiled. "That is refreshing as hell."

Helen pulled a basket of golden brown shrimp out of the fryer and began placing them on a serving platter. "We've got a half bottle left, so I wouldn't worry if I were you. This is a mango aioli, this is an apricot chili dipping sauce, and this is a Maui mustard." She placed some fluffy rice and salad in separate serving bowls, and the women sat down at the dining table. The wine flowed in proportion to the conversation, freely and without abandon. They both came to the conclusion that the white Sancerre was the winning choice, at least with Helen's special shrimp recipe. Yet they finished off the Riesling anyway. After Helen and Judith ate the last bites of dinner, they brought their dishes to the sink, and Judith started wondering if she shouldn't get back to Elaine.

"Now what kind of junk mail did you bring my way? I hope it's not a bill I forgot about," Helen said with a laugh, surveying the envelope that Judith had brought hours ago. Her eyes changed from a smile to concern and back again. "Well, can you beat that?" Helen set the letter on the counter.

"I know it's none of my business, Helen, but after this dinner, I feel like we're old friends. Who is the letter from?"

"That letter is from my best-kept secret. But, what the hell, after all that wine, I feel like spilling my beans. It's from Tracy." Helen set the letter down and walked into her room, returning with a burgundy photo album that had a gold leaf on the front. She opened it, and the first picture was of Helen giving a side hug to a younger woman dressed in academic regalia. "That's her when she graduated."

"Oh my god, you have a daughter!" Judith said, but upon realizing that Tracy was quite white, she wondered if it was an adoption.

"No, no," Helen said with a chuckle. "That's my ex-girlfriend. She's a psychiatrist by now, I imagine. We broke up a couple of years ago. I know, I know, the age difference. That's why we stayed in the closet, so to speak. She's thirty-seven years younger than I am."

"Wow, I'm sorry, I shouldn't have ventured a guess," Judith said as she tried to wipe the shock from her face and polished off the Riesling.

"It's fine. I asked her once why she was attracted to someone as old as I am. And she said she never could do what she was told. She couldn't date men like her mom wanted. She couldn't date people her own age like her dad wanted. She always knew exactly what she wanted—and that's how she got into trouble.

"We met when I was working in Paris, helping curate wine lists for some restaurants prior to their opening. I saw her at a coffee shop, introduced myself, and we talked for hours. Long story short, she was from Miami, and to be honest, my decision to retire here wasn't totally based on being close to my family. It was also to be close to her.

"At first, I was shocked she was interested in me sexually—I'm certainly not filthy rich. But I came to understand that she liked the way I took care of her. We made each other laugh, we gave each other pleasure, and I thought we made a good pair. But she couldn't tell her family about us, and so, ultimately, she called it off. Broke my heart, but I've been through worse. You don't get to be one of the only African American female master sommeliers without any drama."

Judith's eyes were wide.

"So, what could she possibly be writing about?"

"That's what I want to know. Now, Judith, if you'll excuse me, I think I'd better read this letter in private. But thanks for keeping me company. If you ever want to taste more wine with me, you know where to find me."

Judith made her way back to her home, wishing she could stay to hear all of the dirty details about Helen's younger woman instead of spending more time on Betty's death. But Elaine was waiting for her call, and that was reason enough to return.

Chapter Thirteen

Elaine's Shower Scene

E laine was thrilled to finally have planned an event that would get everyone out of their slump—at least, she was at first. She had orchestrated a film festival, where the Secret Pearl residents would watch heady, complex, foreign films together and then discuss their themes and narrative structures. She wanted to do something intellectual, use her brain for once. But when she made her rounds inviting all the ladies, most simply refused to come to her shindig. Elaine was making her last plea at Jo's house, thinking that if Jo would come, so would Brenda, and then she could probably convince the rest.

"Look, Jo, it will be a red-carpet event. Wear your nicest, uh, jeans. I don't think I've ever seen you in anything fancier than jeans, come to think of it. But put on a blouse for fuck's sake. Excuse me, 'for goodness sake' is what I meant to say. But the fashion around here is enough to make me curse. We'll start by watching Akira Kurosawa's *Dreams*, which doesn't so much have a coherent plot as much as many metaphors. Then, after some discussion, we'll move on to *Pi*, by Darren Aronofsky—"

"Sounds great, Elaine, but unfortunately, my mother's coming to visit."

"I haven't even told you the date yet. And I'm fairly sure you aren't on speaking terms with your parents. Didn't they kick you out once they found out you were a lesbian?"

"Look, Elaine, I'm going to level with you. The thing is, your party sounds terrible. I'll go, but only if we can watch *Flashdance*."

"*Flashdance?* But I've already rented Akira Kurosawa's *Dreams* and *Pi.*"

"Well, I have my own copy of *Flashdance*. And I promise the other ladies will come if we watch that instead. I know you think your movies are the intellectual choice, but I think that spending an evening confused is a much dumber idea than watching Jennifer Beals dance." From the look on Jo's face, Elaine could tell that she was serious, and that Elaine wasn't going to win this fight.

"I've never seen *Flashdance.*"

"They pour water on her while she dances, Elaine. Water. While. She. Dances. It's part of the lesbian canon, and if you haven't seen it, then you're the one who needs some culture in your life." Jo's argument was compelling enough to cause Elaine to reconsider.

"Alright, fine. But you have to make sure everyone comes. Tonight at seven in the evening. And try to dress up."

As promised, Jo got all the regular event attendees at the Secret Pearl to the red-carpet *Flashdance* event that Elaine was reluctantly hosting. She had actually rolled out the red carpet that they kept in the utility closet, and she wore an evening gown. She brought all the ingredients for mint juleps, and she prepared canapés, tea sandwiches, and an elegant charcuterie spread, but it seemed a bit much for everyone getting together to watch a blockbuster. Judith dressed up, though Elaine suspected it was just to pacify her.

As the guests arrived, Elaine greeted everyone and showed them to the appetizer table and began to play bartender. Each snack had a label and a cute little bowtie. Even Helen was in attendance, giving Judith a longer and friendlier hug than Elaine would have liked. Elaine wondered why Helen was suddenly attending the events she planned, and whether Judith's presence had anything to do with it.

"What the fuck are tea sandwiches, Elaine?" Brenda asked.

"Just a sophisticated appetizer. Cream cheese and cucumbers are on the left; butter and radish are on the right. Tonight was supposed to be about glamour and intellect, but clearly, it didn't quite turn out the way I planned," Elaine pouted.

"Butter and radish? Are you trying to poison us, Elaine? Thank God Jo brought her chips and bean dip, or we'd all starve!"

"And I brought some PBR, too!" Jo said, to great applause. Elaine ignored this and walked to the front of the room to introduce the film.

"I'm humoring you by showing *Flashdance* tonight," Elaine said, as everyone took their seats. "But this is in no way a sign of my leniency in the future. The next event is going to be as educational as hell. Again, thank you for coming."

"Alright, ladies, let's do our best to not die on the toilet tonight. I think Elaine's sequins will burst off her dress if we ruin another of her events by expiring," Brenda said as the previews began to play.

Elaine dimmed the lights and took a seat.

"This mint julep is delicious. And I'm so excited to see *Flashdance* with you!" Judith squeezed Elaine's hand, which somehow made the event a success already. Then Helen leaned across Judith.

"The tea sandwiches are a delight, Elaine. These would have been perfect with a Chilean Sauv Blanc," Helen said.

As Jennifer Beals biked around town, and Irene Cara's "What a Feeling" began to play, everyone quieted down except for the occasional slurp of beer. And then, suddenly and silently, a smell descended.

"Oh my god, what is that?" Elaine said, jumping up from her seat. "Did someone break wind?"

"Yes, Elaine, it was me. You know I can't have dairy, and yet you keep serving it at your parties. You brought this on yourself," Linda said, not embarrassed in the slightest.

"Next time, make some noise, so we have some warning!" Brenda gasped, plugging her nose and stifling a gag. The potent smell lingered in the room. Elaine made a mental note to herself to find some foods without dairy to serve at her next gathering. It seemed as if this time, Linda wasn't being a hypochondriac about her reaction to dairy; if anything, she had undersold it. The women used pillows to usher the remaining stench out of the theater and into the hallway, and Brenda sprayed some of her perfume in the air.

When everyone was able to comfortably sit down again, Jo started bouncing up and down in her seat.

"This is it! You guys, this is it! This is the scene!" Jo shouted from her seat. Onscreen, Jennifer Beals began her iconic dance. Jo couldn't help herself; she got up and began doing the dance from memory.

"If you really want this to be an authentic re-enactment, Jo," Brenda said, "I can set that scene up for you in the shower. We can dump a bucket of water on your head while you sit on one of those shower stools for the elderly."

"If that's your attempt at showering with me, Brenda," Jo said, "I'll accept your offer." But Jo hadn't paused, even for a moment. When the dance was over, Jo slumped back into her chair, sweaty and spent, with a painful crick in her neck.

"Fine, you sold me on this silly movie. Can we rewind it so we can all try that wet dancing scene?" Elaine asked. Before long, the women were spritzed in water, glowing with sweat, and well aware of how much less coordinated they were than Jennifer Beals.

Chapter Fourteen

Breathless and Wanting

Cynthia sat at Brenda's house, sipping coffee with Jo early one morning while Brenda paged through some of her mail.

"I've got to get my accountant to look at this. My little legal consulting company is taking off, and I'm not sure if an LLC is the best way to go anymore. Cynthia, you're so lucky you're retired. Legal consulting is exhausting. I'm far too old for this shit. I thought this would be an easygoing job, but here I am, day in and day out, working my ass off for people I don't know or care about."

"Yes, sir. Retirement is the life for me," Cynthia said, staring out the window.

"Come to think of it, Cynthia, I've known you for years now, and I don't even know what the fuck you did for a career. Were you a distributor of a not-yet-legal herb? A grower or budtender? A middleman of sorts?"

"No, Brenda. I do other things besides smoke weed."

"Like what?"

"If I told you, you'd never believe me. So, let's just leave it be," Cynthia said with a smirk.

"Oh, no, you're not getting off that easy. Come on, I'll believe you. What were you, an architect? An investment banker?"

"No, don't be silly. You know I hate math. I was a therapist. A sex therapist, actually."

Cynthia continued to stare casually out the window while the other two women exchanged glances. This time it was Jo who spoke up.

"No. Fucking. Way." Jo set her coffee down so abruptly on the table that it splashed up.

"Yes, for thirty-five years, I was a sex therapist, and I made a decent living. I hosted sex therapy retreats, helped couples try naked wellness and find happiness together. It was a fulfilling job. But when my parents died, they left me a small fortune, a very small fortune, but it was enough so that I could retire comfortably. So, I will hopefully never have to work again."

"I would have never guessed in a million years, Cynthia," Jo said, mouth still agape from shock.

"I know. It's hard to believe that I helped people get their lives together, but I did. I was good at it, too."

"Cynthia, you have to come out of retirement, just for one more event. Please? Last time you hosted an event, it turned into an orgy. Your events are giving Elaine's a serious run for their money. I don't know what the hell naked wellness is, but would you consider having an afternoon retreat for Secret Pearl?"

Cynthia considered this for a moment, stirring a bit more cream and sugar into her coffee.

"Okay, I'll do it. But an afternoon session is two-fifty per person." Cynthia smiled. "I'm just kidding. Of course I'll do it, purely for the satisfaction of putting on events that are more interesting than Elaine's."

Cynthia picked the upcoming Saturday for a date, invited all the residents, and set up a scene conducive to therapy. She dotted the event center's floor with yoga mats, lavender aromatherapy (a recent investment, after people complained about the overwhelming smell of patchouli at the orgy), and pillows and blankets. She turned on some music and then thought better of it. *No, what we need now are whale vocalizations*, she thought, so she rummaged through her collection of whale songs.

When everyone arrived, they were all wearing bathrobes and sandals, as they were instructed.

"Welcome, everyone, to the first annual Secret Pearl Sexual Wellness Therapy Session, hosted by Cynthia Chen: me," Cynthia said, wearing a silky red bathrobe and fuzzy red slippers. "Thank you for coming. I hope that we all learn a lot about each other today. Before we get started, please introduce yourself to your neighbors."

The occasion was so popular that some Secret Pearl residents who had never before attended an event showed up. In the front rows were her close friends, though. Elaine was in a slinky, ivory-colored bathrobe, and she sat next to Judith, who was wearing a white spa-like terrycloth bathrobe. Jo wore a no-nonsense flannel bathrobe, and Brenda wore a cozy white bathrobe with her initials monogrammed across the breast. Other women came in wearing everything from Miami Dolphins bathrobes to lacy, teal wraps. Even Wheezer came, surprising everyone in a bright yellow bathrobe with daisies.

"This isn't mine," she said, sensing everyone's confusion at her choice of cheery attire. "I had to borrow this because I'm not the kind of person who spends their afternoons lazing about the house. I'm making an exception, but only because I happen to like the idea of sex therapy."

"Alright, ladies. This afternoon will be unlike any sex therapy that you've ever experienced before. You may disrobe if you wish. I find that being naked helps people view themselves and others without judgment, that it can foster a sense of intimacy and trust. But nudity is not required. And you may leave any time you wish as well. We don't want anyone to feel uncomfortable here."

Cynthia noticed that Brenda was naked by the end of her third sentence. A few others were starting to undress, but most were listening intently.

"Naked therapy was popularized in the nineteen-seventies, which, as you may have guessed, was my favorite decade thus far. And the cornerstone of sex therapy is helping people learn about and articulate their desires, as well as catering to the needs of their partners. Since we have a big group today, we are not going to focus on specific dysfunctions or trauma, but rather have an exploratory time together."

"I have to say I'm a little skeptical," Elaine said, breaking the silence in the room. "What are your qualifications? What is the goal? Is this just going to be another event where you dose us with marijuana and hope it turns out to be a sexual revelation?"

Cynthia had expected Elaine's skepticism and came prepared with an answer.

"I have a master's degree in Sex Therapy, Elaine, and I had to have two-hundred and fifty hours of experience before I could ever work as a therapist, which I then did for thirty-odd years. Naked therapy is good for body image issues, and it's good for post-menopausal women's solidarity. Being naked isn't inherently sexual, but it is natural. Certainly, most therapy doesn't involve nudity. But our meeting today will—if you are inclined. We are going to look at our bodies and accept them for what they are." Elaine seemed to quiet down after Cynthia listed her credentials.

"Accept them? I *adore* our bodies, especially mine," Brenda said with a devilish grin, though she was still the only one naked. "I'm really psychologically advanced, I suppose. Have you ever seen a rack like this on someone over the age of forty?" Brenda threw her shoulders and head back, proudly displaying her chest for all the women to see.

"Yes, Brenda, everyone is extremely impressed by your age-defying rack. But all bodies deserve love and acceptance, not just the ones that are traditionally considered sexy. We are going to start with a meditation that will center our focus on the pelvic bowl. And then we will do vulva mapping.

"But first, we must tend to a little administrative detail. Everyone has informed consent papers to sign underneath your yoga mat. I've invited my colleague, Tonya, a local physical therapist, who can give you a pelvic bowl exam demonstration. She can assess the health of your pelvic bowl and the strength of the muscles inside of you. If you don't want the exam, just don't sign the form. The exam can be performed either vaginally or rectally. Your choice." In walked an attractive woman in her late forties, dressed in a kimono-like bathrobe, and she sat next to Cynthia.

"Both! Is both an option?" Brenda was the first to locate her form and produce a pen from God knows where.

"Hello, everyone. I'm Tonya and I'm here to give a few of you pelvic bowl exams," she said, and everyone raced to find their consent sheets. "I should reiterate—this is purely a physical exam of your pelvic bowl muscles, nothing sexual will happen. I will simply touch you from ribcage to knees, stomach, inner thighs, checking for trigger points, and then I will insert my fingers into your vagina or anus and check your muscle strength. I may need to use a cotton swab to run it up and down your labia to check for sensitivity. But again, this is purely a medical procedure." The Secret Pearl women paused to listen, then rushed once again to complete their forms. Once Cynthia had everyone's signatures, she began her meditation.

"Ladies, lie back and breathe as deeply as is comfortable. Think about a time when you felt disconnected from your vagina."

"Never in my life," Brenda interrupted, as she batted her mascara-laden eyelashes at Tonya.

"Maybe you were told sex was for men. Maybe you were told that vaginas were ugly. But right now, focus on your vagina and thank it for what it has done for you."

"There's not enough time to thank it for everything," Brenda interrupted again.

"Can it, Brenda," Cynthia said. "This is important. Try to be silent, still, and present in the moment. Now slowly relax each part of your body, starting with your head and ending with your toes. Keep those breaths deep and those eyes closed."

Everyone was doing their best to breathe deeply, but Cynthia noticed one or two opening an eye to have a look at Tonya.

"Now, take one of your hands and place it at your heart chakra. Take your other hand and place it at your sacral chakra, otherwise known as your pubic bone. Silently tell your vagina what you love about it. The more at peace you are with yourself and your vagina, the more you'll be able to connect with others."

"Maybe that's what's wrong with Wheezer, she hasn't made peace with her vulva," Brenda whispered.

"My vulva is peaceful enough that it can spend a night alone," Wheezer shot back.

"Your vulva sounds jealous," Brenda replied.

"Ladies, if you're not going to take this seriously, I'm going to have you removed," Cynthia said. "Next, we will do some vulva mapping. Think of the name you like best for your vagina. Is it a pussy? Is it your very own 'secret pearl'? Is it a delicate Georgia O'Keeffe-like flower?"

Brenda stifled a giggle and somehow didn't make a snide comment.

"Touch each place that I mention, and notice all of the sensations, whether they are positive or negative. Start with your hand on your pubic bone, and thank your pubic hair—at least what's left of it—for protecting your vulva. Thank your labia for protecting your vaginal canal. Thank your clitoris for bringing you pleasure. And thank your pelvic bowl for contributing to your sexual health. Now, Tonya, take them through a visual inspection."

Brenda couldn't help but clap her hands and rub them together, and Cynthia rolled her eyes. Brenda never missed an opportunity to be inappropriate.

"If you're comfortable, part your robe and remove your underwear. I have mirrors for anyone interested. If you have vaginal dryness, as many post-menopausal women do, feel free to use some of this lube I brought. Tap your fingers gently around and notice any places of discomfort. Look around the room and see the wide variety of perfectly normal, healthy vulvas."

Cynthia beamed at the ladies, all admiring their vulvas. She had always thought vulvas of all shapes, colors, and sizes were beautiful, and she loved helping others come to the same realization. Brenda was especially encouraging, giving thumbs up and heaps of compliments to the women surrounding her. Her enthusiasm was so overwhelming that a few ladies actually closed their robes.

"Doc, I'm ready for that exam," Brenda said, legs spread and fingers pointing to her vagina. Tonya made her way over and sat down next to Brenda's yoga mat. "I'm Brenda, by the way."

"Hi Brenda. I'm not a doctor, but thank you for allowing me to use you for my demonstration. I'm going to touch you now, to do a quick exam of the tissue surrounding your vulva. Let me know at any point if you're ready to be done with the exam."

"Oh, no, I want the full nine yards, Tonya. Leave no inch unexplored!" Brenda had balled up her bathrobe and was using it as a pillow, lying spread eagle across her yoga mat, as naked as the day she was born. Some women gathered to watch, which seemed to delight Brenda, Cynthia noticed.

"No vaginal dryness here, that's good," Tonya said.

"Damn straight," Brenda said.

"Well, everything on the outside looks healthy. Let me just lube up my gloved finger here, and I'll proceed to the internal portion if that's alright with you."

Cynthia hadn't realized the stir that bringing Tonya would cause, but watching her now, she realized that Tonya *was* alluring. Wheezer licked her lips, watching Tonya inspect Brenda; Judith and Elaine were transfixed, too. Cynthia met Tonya when she needed physical therapy for a twisted ankle, right after she moved to Florida. But she had worked with plenty of physical therapists in her sex practice in Colorado, and Cynthia understood the pelvic bowl work that helped so many women find better sexual health.

But when Cynthia saw Tonya for her ankle, Tonya wore her typical physical therapy clothes, and Cynthia had never noticed her dimples or her long graceful legs. Maybe she had been too professional, Cynthia thought. Maybe she had just been too high. But now that Cynthia was retired, she began to see things more clearly. Tonya had long brown hair that hung to her mid-back, and she had an hourglass figure. She bit her lip when she was concentrating, and someone in the back of the room let out an audible sigh.

"Are you sexually active, Brenda?"

"Yes, I've always heard it's important to use it or lose it." Cynthia saw Tonya's long hair brush across Brenda's thigh and wondered if that tickled.

"Do you know where your G-spot is?"

"No, I think you'd better find it for me," Brenda said, winking at Tonya. Tonya's fingers slid inside Brenda and felt around the territory for a moment. Her thumb was dangerously close to Brenda's clit, and Brenda's sharp intake of breath meant that the placement of her thumb had not escaped Brenda's notice. Everyone watching was silent with anticipation.

"Okay, do you feel that? I am checking that you have sensation everywhere, so you should feel my fingers press on you all of the way from front to back."

Brenda let out a garbled "yep" and closed her eyes tightly. Brenda's face was now beet red; her brow was a bit sweaty. Cynthia noticed that she had started sweating a bit, too.

"That's great. Now, I'm going to pull my fingers upward in a come-hither motion so you can feel that wonderful G-spot place. It's really just the internal portion of the clitoris, and it's an area more than a spot, but you get the idea. Right there, does that feel good?"

"God, yes!" Brenda gasped.

"Great job, Brenda. I have to say, you seem totally healthy to me. We have reached the end of the exam," Tonya said and slipped her fingers out unceremoniously. She checked her watch and raised her eyebrows. "Shit, I'm late."

Brenda sat straight up. "Already? You can't stop now. Are you sure you checked absolutely everything?"

"I sure did. You are as healthy as a horse. But now I have to be off to my next appointment. Thanks for hosting me, ladies!" Tonya got up and tightened her robe, fishing with her toes for her flip-flops. The ladies who were clearly not getting examined began to pout.

"Sorry that I can't stay for more exams. Brenda can probably show you the ropes; otherwise, just give me a call! Cynthia has my number. It's been a pleasure!"

Before too long, the Secret Pearl ladies were mobbing around Cynthia, desperate to get the phone number of the sexy physical therapist who'd left them all breathless and wanting.

Chapter Fifteen

Where's Wheezer?

"L ook, Elaine, I think we should just go check on Wheezer. She's our friend, and she's been acting weird lately," Judith said, pouring another glass of iced tea on an especially warm autumn day. "No one saw her at the Friendsgiving dinner, and no one has seen her since."

"I love that you're willing to give her the benefit of the doubt, but I think you're just unfamiliar with her habits, Judith. This is how Wheezer always acts: standoffish and borderline rude. It's her schtick. Worrying about her will only encourage her, if you ask me."

"I don't care; I'm honestly worried. What if everyone is wrong about Wheezer? She's excluded herself from nearly all of the Secret Pearl activities this month because everyone is treating her like a murderer. And we have no evidence. I understand if you don't want to come along, but I think we should pay her a visit. It's the decent thing to do."

"You know I'll go along if you want me to. I just don't want you to be too terribly upset if there really is a murderer amongst us. Maybe we should bring Jo—she's a black belt, you know. Or Linda. She's surprisingly strong for someone so phobic about everything."

"No, I want to talk to Wheezer on a personal level. No karate, no accusations." The two women finished up their afternoon libations and strolled over to Wheezer's house. They had fallen into a pattern of seeing each other every afternoon, and the visits lasted well into the night. Judith couldn't have been more pleased.

As they held hands and walked along the path, it occurred to Judith that she didn't even know where Wheezer lived, but fortunately Elaine led the way. Elaine seemed to know where everyone lived. Wheezer had one of the nicer residences at the Secret Pearl, nearly as nice as Helen's, Judith supposed. When they walked up to the door, they noticed it was ajar. Judith rang the doorbell, but when no one answered, she peeked inside.

"Hello? Wheezer? It's Judith and Elaine." Judith surreptitiously stepped inside the front door, looking for any sign of Wheezer. She silently hoped this visit wouldn't end up with finding another dead body, but she couldn't think of a good reason the door would be ajar. "Elaine, you wait outside in case there was a break-in."

"No way, Judith. I'm coming in with you."

"Wheezer? Are you home? Wheezer! It's Judith and Elaine. We just wanted to tell you how much we missed you at the Friendsgiving dinner." The two women were inside Wheezer's house now, both holding their breath as they crept along the wall of the entryway.

"Wow, I didn't realize Wheezer's place was so nice. I wonder what she did for a living," Judith whispered, looking at the bespoke furniture and well-appointed kitchen.

"You know, I feel a little guilty that no one here has bothered to really get to know her just because she's grumpy. She must feel so isolated." The women slowly made their way to the back of Wheezer's house, admiring her décor but trying not to be too nosy. They certainly didn't want Wheezer to see them snooping around. When they reached what seemed to be Wheezer's bedroom, Judith gently knocked on the door.

"Wheezer, are you asleep? It's Judith and Elaine." For a moment, there was silence. But a few seconds after, they heard scratching at the door.

"I'm going to open it," Judith said.

"Don't! You know she's in there, and she's going to have us arrested for breaking and entering."

"We didn't break, Elaine, we only entered. Maybe that will mean a lesser sentence." The scratching intensified, and Judith quietly turned the handle and pushed the door open a couple of inches. "Wheezer," she whispered once more before entering.

As the women let themselves in, they found the room empty except for a little black cat. Judith looked at its collar, which simply read "Pants" on the front and had Wheezer's phone number on the back.

"Wheezer and Pants, huh? Do you think they're both asthmatic?" Elaine asked as they tiptoed around like teenagers afraid to wake their parents. They noticed that Wheezer's bed was unmade, and the room was a bit disorganized, but it didn't quite look like a break-in.

"Alright, she's not here. At least we didn't find her dead. Now let's get out of here! Being at a murderer's house is creeping me out," Elaine said, one foot across the threshold to the hallway.

"Look, Elaine," Judith said, something on the nightstand having caught her eye. She picked up a bright yellow, heart-shaped frame with a picture in it. "It's Wheezer and Betty."

Wheezer's arms were fully wrapped around Betty, and Wheezer was smiling so broadly it looked like she might burst with joy.

"I never realized that Wheezer and Betty were *that* close," Elaine said. "That's just more proof. Judith, we have to get out of here!"

"You're right. We're too pretty for jail," joked Judith. "Let's just leave her a note to let her know we stopped by and that we're thinking about her." They walked back into the kitchen, and Judith nosed around for some paper and a pen. She opened a drawer, and at the front was a big, sharp-looking knife, with a sticky note that said: *For Betty.*

"Oh my God, Elaine. Look at this!"

Elaine saw the knife and clasped her hands over her mouth.

"Judith, that seals it! Wheezer killed her. We have to leave before we see anything else, or she'll come after us next!"

"No, we don't even know what the knife means. Let's just try to stay level-headed." Judith eventually saw some paper and a pen next to the refrigerator. She wrote Wheezer a brief note:

Hi Wheezer! Judith and Elaine here. We stopped by because we missed you over the holiday. Your door was open. We hope you're safe and doing well. Let's plan a coffee date soon!

The lightheartedness of the note belied the feeling in Judith's stomach: that Wheezer and Betty were somehow connected, and that something went very wrong. The ladies rushed back to their homes, and Judith cuddled up in bed with her journal. She had to write out her theories about Betty before she started doubting what she just saw.

Chapter Sixteen

Party of Two

It occurred to Elaine that she hadn't planned an event in a while. Cynthia had arranged so many recently that she was encroaching on Elaine's role as the social director of the Secret Pearl, and usually, this would have bothered her. But right now, she was grateful to have the extra time to spend with Judith.

The next event Elaine was planning was a dinner party for the upcoming Friday, and she wanted everything to be perfect. She was going to have the party at her house, and it was going to be the party to end all parties. The theme would be "A Few of My Favorite Things," and it was going to be a Christmas party. She had decorated with raindrops on roses. She'd tried but failed to put extra-long whiskers on Judith's kittens, but she'd invited everyone to bring their pets. They were going to do a secret Santa exchange, and all of the packages were to be wrapped in brown paper and, of course, tied up with strings. She ordered champagne—the good stuff—plus twinkle lights, and made plenty of cute Christmas cookies to snack on.

She had cooked Judith's favorite dishes for the main course. Unfortunately, Judith liked Swedish meatballs with wild rice as a hot dish. Elaine died a little bit inside at the thought of serving a casserole at a fancy party, but Judith was the only person she cared to impress, and so the menu was set.

When the night of the dinner party finally came, Judith showed up first—and last. Though the invitations specifically said to arrive at seven o'clock, sharp (and they also suggested Christmas-themed formal attire, which Elaine fully expected the Secret Pearl ladies would outright ignore), the two women nibbled on appetizers until around seven-thirty, when Elaine finally lost it.

"Is no one coming? I've prepared all this food, and no one even bothered to show up?"

"Well, did anyone RSVP?" Judith gently asked.

"They never RSVP! I eventually quit asking," Elaine said with a sigh.

"Did they say they would come?"

"No, they just gave me their usual complaints. Linda said she was Jewish and uninterested in a Christmas-specific party so late in her life. Jo said she needed to get caught up on her home repairs. Brenda said she wouldn't be caught dead wearing Christmas colors, they don't flatter her complexion, you see. Helen—whom I only invited at your request because she always says no—said she couldn't make it, either. Wheezer rolled her eyes and said she missed the redneck Christmas parties that Betty used to throw, where everyone would line dance. And then she slammed the door in my face, of course. Cynthia said she had another conflicting engagement. Oh my god! Judith, you don't think that Cynthia planned a party at the same time as my party, do you? I tried to book the clubhouse but was told it was unavailable. That bitch!"

"Well, if she did, she didn't invite me," Judith said, sipping champagne. "Why don't we forget about it and just enjoy all this food and champagne ourselves? You decorated beautifully, made all my favorite dishes—I'd hate for this perfect evening to go to waste."

But Elaine was hopping mad now, and she was wearing a path through the living room carpet with all of her pacing. "I was going to have us watch *Citizen Kane*, the best Christmas film of all time! But no, they always want to watch something else, like *Desert Hearts* or *Carol*. You know what we're going to do? We're heading over to that goddamn clubhouse, and we're going to see what kind of hootenanny they're having without us."

If Elaine was swearing, she was mad. She reserved cursing for her foulest moods and her closest friends, just like the good bottle of scotch she had kept so many years at the very back of her liquor cabinet. She grabbed Judith's hand, and they began the short walk to the clubhouse. Palm trees were decorated with Christmas lights, but the festivity only served to remind Elaine what a good time she was supposed to be having right now. As they saw the clubhouse on the horizon, Elaine saw that it was lit up inside.

"Holy dick shitter!" Elaine exclaimed, pointing at the clubhouse.

"What?" Judith asked.

"I'm sorry. I'm not particularly good at swearing. I seldom have occasion to use filthy language."

"In this situation, I'd choose something more along the lines of 'motherfucker,' or 'god damn it,' dear," Judith said. "Hannibird has taught me some obscene phrases. If you're ever in need, I'll just send you a list of what he says when I'm watching scary mysteries."

As they got closer, it was clear: people were rustling around inside the clubhouse. "Son of a fuck monkey," Elaine muttered as she opened the front door to hear some voices inside. "Who the hell is in here, and why wasn't I invited?"

Two men peeked around the corner from the hallway, and Elaine recognized them immediately.

"It's Officers Hank and Jeremy! Don't shoot!" Hank had his hands up until Jeremy jabbed him with an elbow. "We're here on official business."

"Oh, we thought this was a Christmas party. Mind telling us why you're back here?" Judith asked, and Elaine could see how eager she was to get an update on the investigation.

"We're just following up on Betty's death. It's not a murder investigation per se, because we still haven't heard back from the medical examiner. They are so slow. You have to be a real idiot to work at the M.E.'s office," Hank said.

"That's...that's saying something," Elaine said, remembering her unflattering estimation of Hank's intelligence from their first meeting. "So, do you have any leads yet?"

"That's why we're here. We just want to see if we missed anything suspicious. We can't close the place down because it's not technically an investigation, so the murderer could have come back and taken the evidence already."

"Shut up, Hank. Ladies, if you don't mind, we'll get back to looking around," Jeremy said, giving Hank a stern look.

As Judith and Elaine headed back home, Elaine was quiet. She was mad when she believed that Cynthia had the audacity to plan a party at the same time as her get-together, but somehow it was worse that there was no overlapping social event. Her friends just preferred staying home to coming to her meticulously planned events.

When they got back, Elaine's mood had soured considerably. She crumpled on the couch in a dramatic display of disappointment.

"I'm finished throwing parties," Elaine said.

Judith turned the oven on and placed the main courses inside to reheat. She opened a bottle of Elaine's favorite champagne and turned on some Christmas music.

"Come on, Elaine. Your next party will be the best one yet. Maybe you should consider throwing the kind of parties that the other ladies might like, you know, adding some line-dancing into the mix," Judith said as she sat on the couch next to Elaine and rubbed her back.

"No, I mean it. I'm done. You're the only one I wanted to impress with my parties, anyway. Cynthia does a better job, too, she really does. She's unpredictable, but somehow she knows just how to plan something offbeat enough that everyone has a great time. I'm just going to have to find a new hobby."

"I can be your hobby," Judith said with a grin.

"I think I'd like that. I could be a Judith-ologist. Or maybe it's a Judith-onomist," Elaine said, her disappointment disappearing along with the champagne in her glass. The oven beeped, indicating that it was hot enough, and so Judith set a timer, lit some candles, and popped a cookie in her mouth to tide her over. Elaine watched her new lady taking care of her, and realized how nice it felt to be the one who was being coddled, for once.

She thought of her short-lived marriage to Dee, whom she was always caring for, and never the other way around. Elaine was the one consoling Dee about the gambling debt she had hidden before their marriage, researching open relationships so that she could try to give her wife everything she wanted. But when Elaine had a bad day, she was on her own. Dee was a few years younger than Elaine, a professor, and she was as funny and charming as she was adorable. But the relationship was one-sided, and when it became evident to Elaine that an open relationship was not doable, it was over. Elaine left, and Dee never tried to win her back. She only saw Dee once after that, when they signed their divorce papers. It was as if the relationship hadn't even happened; all of their intimacy just vanished into thin air overnight.

If Elaine was honest, maybe that's why she liked to plan events in the first place. Though the wedding had turned out poorly after Dee had too much to drink, it was still the highlight of their relationship. The wedding was so beautiful; Elaine had planned every last detail to perfection. All of their friends came and were so impressed by this marriage of the minds: a professor and an engineer. *What a power couple,* they all thought, or, at least, that's what Elaine imagined they thought. Elaine and Dee bonded over which flowers and which hilariously vaginal appetizers to select (oysters, of course, pistachios, tortellini specially shaped for them, and fortune cookies), and they had so much fun planning for the big event. They looked gorgeous, Elaine in her gown and Dee in her dapper tuxedo. For a moment, they were the perfect couple.

Elaine thought that maybe she stopped her search for happiness and settled instead for appearing successful, putting on posh events and rolling her eyes at anyone not sophisticated enough to enjoy them. All of that seemed silly now that she had Judith. Judith was even a good enough sport that she wore a lovely red pantsuit to the party, fitting Elaine's theme perfectly. Her crazy hair was gathered at the nape of her neck, and she looked utterly delicious as she licked the icing off her fingers from the cookie she thought she snuck undetected.

Elaine's attraction to women had changed as she aged. No longer did she flock to the woman with the most sculpted body as Brenda seemed to, and her head didn't turn anymore when good-looking twenty-somethings crossed her field of view. The wrinkles around Judith's kind eyes were what sent her into a dripping, wet mess these days—though the wet part was becoming rarer as the years ticked by. Of course, Judith's perfect, gravity-defying ass did not hurt one bit, but that wasn't even close to the first thing Elaine noticed; Elaine noticed her ass well after she had realized she was taken with Judith. Well, at least a couple of minutes after.

Judith's perfect ass was now in Elaine's view as she bent over to check the contents of the oven.

"I'm going to take these out; they're bubbling. We should probably let them sit for just a minute," Judith said as she poked around in drawers until she stumbled upon oven mitts.

"Perfect. I want a few minutes with you before we eat," Elaine said, and Judith looked up at her and grinned. Judith had a way of reading Elaine's mind, already knowing what Elaine was thinking.

Judith sauntered over toward Elaine, doing a slow, sexy catwalk to the rhythm of "Oh Holy Night" that played in the background. Her strut was over the top and a little out of character for Judith, which was precisely why Elaine loved it when Judith had a glass of something. She was bold and silly, and her Midwestern manners flew right out the window. "How about I peel you out of that pantsuit, and we eat dinner naked?"

"Sounds like a party to me," Judith said, dropping her blazer on the floor. "Peel away."

Elaine undid her red belt, giving it a good snap before tossing it aside. She pulled Judith's blouse from her midriff, unzipped her pants, and Judith shimmied a bit before she pulled at her panties until they sat around her ankles. Seeing Judith naked made it clear to Elaine that their dinner was about to get cold again.

Judith stood and leaned over Elaine, tugging at the zipper on her elm green, sequined gown. Elaine shrugged her shoulders and stood, leaving the gown on the floor. It may as well have been Christmas already, for Elaine. The thrill of being with Judith was palpable, someone who liked Elaine when she was unlikeable, someone who wanted her even when she didn't want to be herself anymore. It was a minor thing, to throw an unattended party, but it made Elaine crave the reassurance that Judith's naked and waiting body would give her. Elaine made space for Judith to lie back on the couch. She buried her face between her legs and stayed there until she made Judith feel as warm and loved as Judith had made her feel that night.

"I don't want to be your hobby," Judith said after she regained her composure. "I want to be your full-time job." She smiled that mischievous smile at Elaine, and the two wandered, naked, into the kitchen to pick at the now cold hot dishes.

"Casserole is objectively the worst food," Elaine said, grinning.

"You're wrong there, honey. Casserole is the pinnacle of opulence," Judith said, and they both laughed.

Chapter Seventeen

Oh, the Huge Manatee

I can't believe I had to get up at five-thirty in the morning for this shit," Brenda said, climbing into the van that was headed to their next adventure.

"That doesn't sound like 'Happy Birthday' to me," Cynthia said. Cynthia had planned the event as her own birthday celebration. She bought everyone tickets to go snorkeling with manatees, which initially sounded like fun to Brenda. She neglected to mention that their tour was at seven in the morning, and they had to get there half an hour early to squeeze themselves into wetsuits. "Alright, roll call! Linda!"

"Here," Linda said, taking a puff of her inhaler.

"Brenda," Cynthia said.

"Here," Brenda grumbled. "And so is Martina, my lady friend." A few heads turned to see Martina, a younger Hispanic woman with her arm draped around Brenda.

"Judith and Elaine?"

"Here," the twosome chimed in, a little bit too cheerfully for this early in the morning, to Brenda's mind.

"Jo?"

There was a momentary silence until Brenda saw out of the corner of her eye Jo walking slowly across the sidewalk and clutching her back. She stuck her head out the van window to signal her.

"Jo? Are you limping? What's the matter? Did you try to have acrobatic sex again?"

A sheepish smile crossed Jo's face as she eventually reached the van. "You know me too well, Brenda."

"Well? Come on! Who is she?" Brenda pried.

"A lady never tells," Jo said, trying her best to look demure.

"No one's ever accused you of being ladylike before," Brenda said, a bit wounded that she wouldn't be privy to the details. Jo carefully made her way into the car, sitting up painfully straight and wincing. "Are you sure you're going to be up for snorkeling, Jo?"

"Oh, sure. I took some Ibuprofen and rubbed on some Bengay. I just need a minute."

"You know, Jo, if you're feeling terrible, I've got something that will fix you right up—" Cynthia began.

"Let me stop you right there, birthday girl. I'm not getting high before we swim with sea monsters. That wouldn't end well," Jo said, rolling her head around her shoulders in gentle circles.

"You guys are no fun at all. Anyway, Wheezer?"

Silence filled the van.

"Wheezer's not coming, Cynthia. She never does anymore. Not since the murd-" Brenda stopped herself. She didn't want to have to explain Betty's death to Martina.

"Maybe I should knock on her door and make sure she's okay," Judith said.

"Absolutely not! I got up at five-fucking-thirty. Five-fucking-thirty in the morning! And if we miss our tour, Wheezer won't be the only murderer amongst us." Brenda knew she was bad at keeping secrets. She had only managed not to mention the suspicious death for about ten seconds. Still, it was a personal record.

"Okay, let's get going! Who's driving?" Cynthia asked, realizing everyone had already situated themselves in the back. "Can't be me, ladies. You don't want me driving. I've been high since last night, and I'm not stopping now. It's my birthday!"

Judith and Elaine unbuckled, and Judith took the driver's seat. Elaine pulled up directions, and the ladies were on their way.

"Alright, everybody! Let's go see some big fat sea cows!" Cynthia said, clasping her hands together.

"I'll blend right in with the sea cows, once I put on my wetsuit," Brenda lamented.

Brenda pulled out her latest cross-stitch endeavor. This one read: *Buckle Up Buttercup, There's Fuckery to Spread.*

"Mi amor, can you tell me what 'fuckery' means? I have never heard it before," Martina said, pointing to Brenda's craft.

"Fuckery is when you do something fucked up, like nonsense, or bullshit. It's a quintessential English word. See? I told you this field trip would be educational, mi bonita," Brenda said.

Jo leaned over and extended her hand. "I'm Jo! And you are?" Brenda couldn't be sure, but she thought she detected a hair of possessiveness in Jo's voice. *Serves her right, after sleeping with someone new and not even clueing me in,* thought Brenda.

"Nice to meet you, Jo. I'm Martina, Brenda's girlfriend." Brenda coughed a little when Martina said this.

"She's from Ensenada, and she's brilliant," Brenda bragged. "She knows how to say 'I have a headache' in three different languages."

"But you like it when I whisper in your ear those Latin words of love," Martina protested.

"That's because I can't hear you otherwise," Brenda said. "Speaking of things I can't hear, Linda, you're awfully quiet this morning."

"That's because I have laryngitis," Linda whispered hoarsely. "I haven't been to the doctor yet, but it could be cancer. Throat cancer."

"Now, don't strain yourself, Linda. If your body doesn't want you to talk, you better listen to it and keep your mouth shut," Brenda said.

Before too long, they had arrived for their tour. With some difficulty, the women pulled on their neoprene suits and got situated on the boat.

"Won't it be cold, swimming in the winter?" Judith wondered aloud.

"No, swimming in Florida in the winter is probably warmer than swimming at the Minnesota lake in July. On second thought, this is a river, so it might be chilly," Elaine replied.

"I'm worried the manatee will bite me," Martina added with a twinge of embarrassment.

"No, dear, the manatees are vegetarians. They don't eat anything but plants."

"Just like me!" Cynthia chimed in.

"Can it, Cynthia," Brenda said. "The only thing worse than being up at five-thirty in the morning is having to hear you proselytize about veganism."

"You have to be nice to me on my birthday," Cynthia said. "I bought your ticket and rented the van, and so help me God, I will leave you here."

"Alright. I'll be nice today. And you're right—the manatees are a lot like us. They're chubby, and they have whiskers," Brenda said as she ran her fingers over her upper lip.

The ladies took a short boat ride to the river where the manatees were supposed to congregate during the winter. Even in a wetsuit, it was hard not to notice how sexy Martina was. She had a slight build with short, dark hair, but was in particularly good shape—an athlete, just like Brenda preferred. Her full red lips were the only feminine thing about her. Some women let out an audible sigh of disappointment when Martina's body disappeared under the water.

The women quietly waited in the water, just as they had been instructed to do by the captain. Slowly and intermittently, manatees hesitantly surfaced, but it was Martina who held the ladies' attention.

"Martina, if you need help climbing out of that wetsuit, I'm your gal," Linda whispered hoarsely, hoping that Brenda couldn't hear her.

"I may not have the best hearing, Linda, but I have unbelievable intuition when someone is trying to engage in fuckery with my lady friend," Brenda said, swimming in between Linda and Martina.

"How you manage to look so good in a wetsuit, mask, and snorkel is beyond me," Judith said, surprising herself.

"Really, Judith? You, too?" Elaine asked.

"She's just young, is all. Ah, to be forty again. And Elaine, I wouldn't have said a word if I didn't know how confident you are in our relationship," Judith said, but Elaine playfully dunked her under water.

"Look, if anyone is helping her out of her wetsuit, it's me. It's my effing birthday!" Cynthia said, wanting to join in the fun. "Look how slow that manatee is swimming!" She pointed to some clear water nearby.

"That looks like Jo trying to get to the van this morning," Brenda said with a laugh. "Don't think you're going to get away without telling me who your new love interest is."

Suddenly, bubbles began to surface around Linda.

"Linda, for God's sake. Can't you hold it in? We're in public, with my new girlfriend," Brenda complained.

"She rejected me. Why should I give myself a stomachache?" Linda said, grinning with satisfaction.

One giant manatee surfaced and began to nuzzle Martina. "Oh, te amo! Que hermosa," she said.

"Even the wildlife thinks my lady is hot," Brenda said.

Judith kept chiming in with facts about the manatees, and, aside from Martina, was the most popular with the gentle giants. She seemed to have a way with animals that the rest of the ladies simply did not. The three-hour tour was over before any of the ladies were ready. Brenda made sure that no one helped Martina out of her wetsuit and stood guard while she finished dressing. The ladies returned to the van, happy and exhausted, and made a quick pit stop for key lime pie and coffee before returning home.

"Alright, I admit it, Cynthia. That was worth waking up early for," Brenda said before diving into her creamy green treat. "And I didn't think about murder even once!"

"Then why do you keep bringing it up, loca?" Martina asked in between bites.

"Well, I didn't want to tell you because I didn't want to worry you. But one of the ladies at the Secret Pearl died rather suddenly, and there very well could be a murderer in our midst."

"Seems like a stretch to me."

"We're aging, Martina! Don't begrudge us the one bit of juicy gossip that's happened this year."

"Oh, now, don't sell us short," Jo said with an evil grin. "I happen to have it on good authority that one of the ladies at the Secret Pearl—in our tight-knit friend group, no less—is dating a..." Jo took a moment to look Brenda directly in the eyes. "A man."

Everyone's eyes widened as Brenda's fork clattered on her plate. Brenda's phone buzzed in her pocket, and she sneakily pulled it out to see a new text from Jo:

You can keep secrets from me, but I can keep secrets from you, too.

Brenda huffed and slipped the phone back into her pocket without saying a word.

Chapter Eighteen

Casseroles and Confession

C ynthia had planned a quick brunch at the clubhouse on a sunny Saturday morning, just to say goodbye to everyone before she left for a brief visit to her family in Colorado. Wheezer had, as she always did, begged off. This morning, however, Elaine and Judith still showed up on Wheezer's doorstep that morning, asking her to join them.

"I already told Cynthia 'no,' and I'm not afraid to tell you 'no,' too," Wheezer said as soon as she opened her front door. "It's impolite to show up to a gathering after you've RSVP'd your regrets, and you motherfuckers know I'd hate to be impolite."

"But we're worried about you, Wheezer! You haven't come to anything lately, and I'm disappointed I haven't gotten to know you better yet. Plus, there will be plenty of food; I'm sure of it. Look, I brought my egg bake," Judith said, offering the lidded pan in her oven-mitted hands as evidence of the bounty.

"It's a casserole," Elaine said, looking disappointed.

"No, I don't think it's a good idea. Everyone has been pretty terrible to me since Betty's passing—you have to admit it. I've never been close with anyone here, but now I'm an outcast."

"But that's the thing, Wheezer. They think you did it. Whenever you don't show up, they talk about how suspicious it is that you're hiding. Showing up might at least temporarily halt the gossip."

"Will there be booze?" Wheezer asked, seeming surprised that she was considering their invitation.

"Yes, as a matter of fact. I brought champagne and orange juice for mimosas," Elaine said.

"Fine. But I'm only coming for the mimosas, and I'm leaving as soon as I'm drunk," Wheezer said.

Judith took this as a victory. "Great! We'll all be together again, finally."

"You sound like a fucking Hallmark movie," Wheezer replied.

As the women neared the clubhouse, they could see it was already buzzing with activity. Women brought their favorite brunch dishes and displayed them on a long table against the wall. Linda was pacing the table and shaking her head.

"Only half of these are labeled. How am I supposed to tell if I'm allergic to these dishes if I have to guess what they are?"

"It's fucking rude, that's what it is," Wheezer said, looking happy to have someone nearby who also was in a bad mood.

"You're damn right it is. I guarantee, even though it's brunch, at least half of these have shrimp in them. Shrimp! For brunch! What the hell is wrong with Floridians?" Linda used a gloved hand to open some of the lids, smell, and shake her head some more.

"Aren't you from here?"

"No, I'm from New York," Linda said.

"No shit. Me, too. How have we been neighbors for this long without once having a meaningful conversation?" Wheezer said.

"I don't know," Linda said. "But I can tell you this would never pass for brunch in New York. Nobody brought a bagel. Not one person."

"And if they had, it would have been a shrimp-flavored bagel," Wheezer said.

Linda burst out laughing. "You're absolutely right."

"Well, well, well. Wheezer made a friend. Don't be seduced by her charm, Linda, or you might end up like Betty," Brenda said.

"Oh, come on. You don't honestly believe Wheezer did it, now do you?" Linda asked, suddenly uncomfortable.

"I wouldn't risk it, sweetie," Brenda said. "Let's put it to a vote. Who here thinks Wheezer killed Betty," Brenda yelled, summoning everyone's attention. Several hands shot up, and Wheezer balled her fists up with frustration.

"You know what, Brenda? I can't take it anymore. You don't like me, so I must have killed someone, right? You'd make a terrible detective. Anyway, let's just settle this once and for all. Attention, attention," Wheezer tapped on her glass lightly with her spoon, quieting the few conversations that had sprung up. "I just wanted to confess to everyone at brunch today. You really have me pegged. I killed Betty. I did it! I murdered her on the toilet! Okay? Any questions before I turn myself in?" Wheezer's voice dripped with sarcasm.

To everyone's horror, Officer Hank poked his head into the doorway and waved to the women.

"Fucking hell!" Wheezer said. "Was this a setup? Judith? Elaine? Is that why you brought me here?"

"God, no! We had no idea you were going to confess," Judith said earnestly.

Hank finally spoke up. "No, no. No one called me here today. I just came around with Officer Jeremy the other night to do some poking around and, wouldn't you know it, I lost my checkbook. I thought maybe I'd left it somewhere around the pool. So, I came by to see if it was still here. Lucky me!" Officer Hank put his checkbook back into his pocket. "But Wheezer, is it? I think I'm going to have to bring you down to the station for questioning."

"Really, Officer? But has anyone even determined that Betty was murdered?" Wheezer asked, her voice taking on a chilling calm.

"No, not yet. I can hold you for seventy-two hours before I have to charge you, though. And if I didn't bring you down, I have a feeling Jeremy will get all pissy with me again."

Wheezer fished her keys out of her pocket and threw them unceremoniously at Judith.

"Judith, will you take care of my cat while I'm gone? You owe me. You got me into this fine mess," Wheezer said. And with that, she disappeared from the Secret Pearl.

Chapter Nineteen

———————●———————

A Really Sharp Knife

S he asked you to pet sit, not house sit," Elaine complained as
Judith put together a small bag of things to stay at Wheezer's
for a while, shortly after the catastrophic brunch.

"Yes, she did. But she also said I got her into this mess, which is
true. I made her come to that brunch. I had no idea the cops would
be there! We have to look around, find something that could clear her.
It's the least I can do," Judith said. "We have to start giving her the
benefit of the doubt. No one else is."

"Do you honestly think that Wheezer is going to think that you,
rummaging around her house, uninvited, for a few days is a favor?
She's going to be pissed when she finds out."

"Not if I find something that could help her!" Judith said with a
look on her face that clearly showed her mind was made up.

"So, are we going to go over there and get rid of the knife that
has a threatening message for Betty? Or are we only doing slightly
illegal things? I need to know exactly what I'm getting myself into
here. Maybe I should call Brenda and use her lawyerly wisdom. She
could help us stay out of jail, maybe. Come to think of it, I have no
idea what kind of law she practiced."

"No, we're not calling Brenda. She has no interest in helping
Wheezer—she's always the one antagonizing her. And of course
I won't get rid of the knife. I'm not trying to clear Wheezer if she
actually killed Betty, I'm just doing my due diligence. I'm all packed.

If you don't want to help, I won't blame you. But I'm going to look around," Judith said as she zipped up her small bag.

"Are you always this nosy?" Elaine asked, taking Judith's hand in hers.

"Oh, for the love of Jane Lynch, I'm not nosy. I'm inquisitive. It's why I was a good vet. I like to get to the bottom of things, and I hate to see an injustice done—let alone an injustice I'm responsible for. Now, are you coming or not?"

"You know I'll come with you," Elaine said, and the women were off to Wheezer's home. When they reached her place, Judith unlocked the door and brought her bag to Wheezer's room. It was still a bit disorganized, and Judith's eye was drawn instantly to the yellow-framed picture of Betty and Wheezer, embracing.

"She's not much of a bed-maker," Judith said, putting her sleeping bag on the floor. Pants, Wheezer's cat, was not in the room, and so Judith began cleaning out the litter box that sat near the washing machine in a small closet just outside Wheezer's bedroom. She refilled the food and water bowls in the kitchen, each custom-made with a cute little drawing of pants.

"Pants, where are you, girl?" Judith asked as Elaine relaxed on the lanai with the newspaper. "I'm here to take care of you while your mom's away. But don't worry, we'll bring her home just as soon as we can."

The cat appeared, with a squeaky toy in its mouth that it presented as a trophy to Judith. It was a stuffed pair of yellow pants.

"You're friendly, aren't you? Just like my Clawdia. You've got to help me find something that can help prove your mom isn't guilty. She's not, is she? You seem pretty pampered to me, and I always judge people by how they treat their pets. You're not a murderer's baby, are you?" She looked over at Elaine, reading the obituaries in the newspaper. "Aren't you going to help me search this place?"

"I can't leave my post, Judith. I'm your lookout. I'm just here to keep you out of trouble," Elaine said, not glancing up from the paper. "And I wouldn't say no to a glass of wine, since you're in the kitchen."

Judith sighed. She didn't know when they had turned into an old married couple, but it seemed they already had. She glanced at the clock; it was nearly five o'clock, so she decided there would be no harm in opening the bar. She went back to Wheezer's bedroom to grab the bottle she'd brought over and saw the picture again. Something about it struck her as odd. Why would Wheezer keep it on display, if she had hated Betty enough to kill her? Judith picked up the frame to study it again and sat on Wheezer's messy bed. As she held it, she decided to open the frame to check for a date written on the back of the photo, something Judith's mom had always done with their family pictures. But as she unhooked the back of the deep frame, some papers fell out.

The papers were meticulously folded, well read, and well cared for. Not a wrinkle could be found, but the creases had been folded so often that the papers collapsed in spots. Judith, feeling a twinge of guilt, opened up the paper and began to read it.

Wheezer,
You already know how much I love you. The past few months have easily been the best of my life. I hope you feel the same way. I love you more than gardening, and I love you more than line-dancing. But I think you already know what I'm about to say.
I know that you will call me a coward for writing you a letter rather than talking to you in person. But I know that if I speak to you in person, we will have a fight where we both say things we don't want to remember saying and hear things we don't want to remember hearing. Instead, I'd rather talk about the things I do want to remember.
I want to remember the look on your face when I told you I loved you for the first time. Your response? "Stop fucking around." Classic Wheezer. But I wasn't fucking around, was I?
I want to remember the first weekend we went away together. I don't need to say much more to jog your memory, hopefully, because I won't forget a single moment. Plus, the things we did are unmentionable in polite company.
I want to remember when you read me that one poem by Audre Lorde for the first time—how you were the first to get me reading poetry. I still remember each line. No one else knows the Wheezer who reads poetry. Just me. At least, that's what you said. I want to remember that.
I want to go forward, bringing all these happy memories with me, and leaving behind the negativity that grows each time we see each other. "Everything has an expiration date,"—that's something you always say, especially when people die. I tend to agree. I don't want to taint the beautiful relationship we've had with what we've become: a bickering, unhappy couple.
I know you think I'm not being faithful to you, and I want to give

you the peace of mind that you deserve. I'm not cheating on you. Never have, never would. To be frank, I think you overestimate my desirability by several orders of magnitude. Every time we would sit down to eat dinner at a restaurant and a beautiful woman would enter, you thought she was hot on my trail. It was flattering, at first, to have someone find me so alluring. No one has ever thought I was as irresistible as you did, and I thank you for that.

Anyway, this letter sets both of us free to enjoy the happy memories we have of one another so that we don't have to throw away old pictures, stamp out painful memories, and avoid each other at parties. Instead, we can just share a fondness of something that was perfect for a time.
Love,
Betty

Judith sat for a moment. They *were* in love, she thought. She knew that love was frequently a motive for murder, but the letter didn't sound like the acrimonious break-up letter she would expect to find if Wheezer had been a murderer. Guiltily, she unfolded the paper behind it to continue reading.

Betty,
I honestly don't know what to say. I can't say your letter came as a surprise, but the lack of shock didn't lessen the sting or the finality of what you had to say. I knew from the start that I was lucky to have you, and that, eventually, you would realize how out of my league you are. I respect the fact that you have recognized this and are moving on. I also appreciate that we won't end our relationship with one last fight. You're right. If you had come over to tell me this, there would have been yelling. Yelling and possibly crying. You would tell me what a jealous wretch I am, and I would shout about how reckless you are with money, your terrible gambling problem, your needless plastic surgery. I guess I'm doing that now, getting my last digs in before I become irrelevant to you.

Before you go, I want to give you a parting gift. It's not a last attempt to get back together or something to make you feel guilty, believe me. But I know you have no spare cash right now and that you've wanted a first-rate knife for a while so that you can take your professional-level baking skills and see how they translate into the world of cooking. I

have no doubt you will be an overnight success. As soon as I gather my nerve, I'll deliver this letter and the present to you. I haven't wrapped it quite yet, but I should apologize in advance for my wrapping skills. My surgeon's fingers somehow don't have the patience to make a gift look neat and pretty.
All my love,
Wheezer

P.S. I will keep all of the yellow things you have bought me, and they will always remind me of you. A small pop of color in my otherwise greyscale life.

"Judith? Are you waiting for the wine to age, dear? I honestly don't care that much and would prefer a lesser glass now, to a fully ripened one in five years' time, my darling," Elaine yelled from the lanai.

Judith paused for a moment. She felt bad enough knowing this personal information about Wheezer herself, so she didn't want to share it with Elaine. She grabbed the bottle of Beaujolais and returned to the kitchen, but, of course, she had forgotten a wine opener. She rummaged around in the kitchen drawers and saw the knife with the note on it. She wished she could hide it or get rid of it, but Wheezer would undoubtedly notice. *Why hadn't Wheezer been more careful*, wondered Judith. But it was all too obvious. She wasn't getting rid of any evidence because she hadn't killed Betty. After a minute more of hunting around, Judith produced a wine opener and two glasses full of Beaujolais, and she was more than ready to sit on the lanai and relax with Elaine.

"Where were you, Jud?" Elaine said as she folded up the paper and tossed it onto the coffee table.

"I just got lost in my thoughts, I guess." Judith extended the glass of wine as a peace offering for taking so long. "The more I think about it, the more I am positive that Wheezer didn't kill Betty. We have to get her out of jail. We have a moral obligation."

"What about the knife we found?" Elaine asked, taking a sip, looking pleasantly surprised, and then checking the label on the wine bottle.

"I'm guessing it was a gift."

"Yeah, a really sharp knife. What a normal, non-threatening gift."

"Well, Betty did love to bake. That's what everybody says," Judith said.

"It doesn't take a really sharp knife to cut a muffin."

"If Wheezer killed her, why not dispose of the weird gift, then? It just doesn't make sense she'd leave it in the drawer. It's too suspicious."

"So you agree it's suspicious?"

"I think it's a gift, and I think Wheezer had nothing to do with Betty's death. That's all."

Pants had curled up in Elaine's lap and was taking a brief nap in a rapidly fading sunbeam. A pang of longing for her own pets sprung up in Judith, silly as she knew it was. Sometimes she missed them even if she hadn't seen them for just one day. They had always been what she loved the most, and it felt strange that Elaine now inhabited that spot. Strange, but lovely. She wondered what horrifying string of words Hannibird was putting together, and whether Cat Benatar had fallen asleep in her laundry hamper again, as she was known to do. "Elaine, would you do me a huge favor? I mean, really huge," Judith said, and tried but failed to bat her eyelashes. She had never been good at looking cute to get her way.

"Anything for you, my love," Elaine said, tucking the tail of her grey bob behind her ear.

"Will you throw another party? Now, before you say no, I just want you to hear me out. I think we need to get everyone together to question them. If Wheezer didn't do it, maybe somebody else did. Brenda, for instance. She's been so quick to be judge, jury, and executioner for Wheezer—it's a pretty great way to keep the investigation from pointing to her," Judith spoke quickly as if her voice was bracing for impact.

"Absolutely not. Nope. I've hung up my party-throwing hat, Jud. You know that. Anyway, it would be futile. People didn't come to my party when I tried to make it fun. What should I say for this get-together? Hello, friends. Please come over to my house to be questioned by my girlfriend, who is conducting an amateur crime investigation for a death that may have been due to natural causes? I have a hunch that no one will show up, Judith." Elaine only called Judith by her full name anymore when she meant business, so Judith knew this would be an uphill battle.

"Okay, I'll do all the planning, you'll just be the face of the event. I'm still new here, but everyone loves you. I'll cook everything, clean, I'll buy all the booze—we'll even have it at my place. And then we'll sneak in some questions about Betty's murder, casually."

"I don't know. It sounds like a terrible idea to me. I'm still mad about the Christmas party, Judith!" Elaine sat her wine down on the table so abruptly that some sloshed over the side.

"Please? Pretty please?" Elaine was unmoved. Judith sighed. "Okay, I was going to save this for something special, but I'll let you try the scarves and role playing, like you mentioned. It may not work out well, but I'll give it a go."

At this, Elaine paused.

"Alright. Fine. But don't blame me if no one shows up. So, what kind of party do you think we should plan?"

Judith smiled wildly. "A slumber party!"

"Oh, Judith. You're killing me," Elaine said, but she showed no sign of undoing their bargain.

Chapter Twenty

Truth or Dare

As promised, Elaine was going door to door, inviting the Secret Pearl crew to the slumber party.

"A slumber party, huh? But that sounds like fun. Why are you hosting an event that will be fun?" Jo said.

"Ha, ha. Are you fucking coming or not?"

"Jesus, Elaine, why the hostility?"

"You didn't show up for my Christmas party. I had to eat enough appetizers to serve twenty-five people because no one came. No one, Jo. I was eating baked brie for breakfast. Swedish meatballs for snacks. A garlic bread Christmas tree for dessert. I've never been so constipated in my whole life," Elaine said, staring daggers at Jo.

"So you finally came to your senses, and you're going to plan a party that everyone will appreciate?" Jo was clearly not going to let up on the taunting. But that was fine with Elaine. *Just think of the scarves and some light bondage,* she thought, determined to finish the rounds of invitations.

"Yes, Jo, I've come to my senses. You and everyone else were so right about everything. From now on, I'm drinking PBR and learning to play pool. Thank you for drilling some common sense into me," Elaine muttered through clenched teeth.

"If I didn't know better, I'd think you were being sarcastic," Jo said as she tossed the empty PBR can she was holding into the recycling bin. "But you know what? Shockingly, a slumber party sounds like a great time. Count me in."

Elaine already had her notebook out and was in the process of crossing Jo's name off the list.

"Sorry you can't make it," she said before replaying Jo's response in her head. "Wait, you're going to come?"

"Yeah, I will. I haven't been to a slumber party in decades. Are we going to paint each other's toenails? I mean, not my toenails, of course, unless it's clear polish. Have a pillow fight? Use a Ouija board? I can bring my copy of *Flashdance* in case anyone is up for a second viewing. This is going to be great, Elaine!"

Elaine had to admit she felt a little disappointed in how excited Jo had been for this party. There wouldn't be themed cocktails or anyone dressed formally, just a bunch of her friends in pajamas playing games. Now that she thought about it, she saw how the party could be considered slightly appealing. Brenda said she would come because Martina had recently broken up with her, and she had a free night for plans. Linda agreed to attend if Elaine could ensure that no one would bring feather pillows or down bedding because her allergies would flare up, and she didn't want to get another sinus infection. Cynthia was the only one left.

"I'll be there! You know I like to party. And by party, I mean take naps. So this is the best of both worlds for me! I'll bring brownies."

"No need, Cynthia. We have the food taken care of."

"I'll bring them, just in case," Cynthia said. "I'll bring my Ouija board, too. I know Jo wants to give that thing a try. This is going to be so much fun! See, Elaine? I knew you could plan a fun party."

It took all Elaine's strength to smile and head back to Judith's house, where Judith was busily preparing a list of questions for her suspects.

"Well, everyone said they'd come, not that we can take their word for it," Elaine said. "Even Helen! But I think she's just coming because she has a little crush on you. As soon as I said you were behind the idea, she couldn't RSVP fast enough."

"Oh, Elaine. I'm sorry this party is putting you in such a mood. But you have nothing to worry about; Helen and I are just friends. She's a sommelier and a hell of a cook. I'd be an idiot not to be friends with her. Come to think of it, maybe I'll ask if she can bring that delicious coconut shrimp she made for me. It was so good I have wet dreams about it. Well, okay, maybe they're more like dry dreams now, but when I was a teen, they were wet."

"Linda can't have shrimp," Elaine said, resting her elbow on the kitchen counter and her chin in her palm. "I mean, I don't personally care, but I'd rather save myself the trouble of listening to her bitch all night."

"Ugh, that's right. I'll just make some nachos then. Everybody loves nachos, right?"

Elaine shrugged. She hated to be such a party pooper, but she felt bitter about the Christmas party, still. She wanted Judith's investigation to be over so they could spend all their time in bed together.

When the night of the party finally rolled around, Elaine couldn't wait for it to be over. Judith's home was decorated with flashlights, books full of horror stories, hypoallergenic pillows everywhere, and board games. The kitchen table was chockablock with popcorn, nachos, cheap beer, wine, and Cynthia's brownies. Judith had wisely put a warning on the brownie label: "Cynthia's famous fudge brownies. Beware: these have weed in them no matter what Cynthia says. Imbibe at your own risk."

As people trickled in, Hannibird became more animated, swiveling his head around.

"Not these bastards again," he squawked.

"Come on, Hannibird, let's be good hosts," Judith chastised.

Judith wasn't wearing sweats, like Elaine thought she might be, but was in a cute pink and white striped poplin shirt and shorts. Elaine wore her silk black and gold kimono, which she typically reserved for special evenings. Jo wore an old Miami Dolphins tee-shirt with matching sweatpants, and Cynthia showed up in a well-worn "I'm With Her" tee-shirt and soft pants with a psychedelic neon print. Brenda wore a white bathrobe with what seemed like nothing underneath. Helen was wearing navy flannel L.L.Bean pajamas, which seemed a bit warm, but Elaine tried her best to reserve judgment. The fashion around her felt a bit much to take in, so she decided to help herself to one of the brownies in the kitchen. She'd never been interested in marijuana, but she thought that maybe the brownie would help her chill out and get through the evening without accosting anyone for blowing off her party.

As everyone enjoyed appetizers and a few drinks, Judith made her move. "Anyone up for a good, old-fashioned game of Truth or Dare?"

"I was born ready!" Brenda shouted before anyone else could respond. The women gathered around the kitchen table and squabbled over who would go first. Judith won the popular vote since the party was at her house.

"Clusterfuck! This is a clusterfuck," Hannibird chimed in from his cage. Elaine had to agree.

"Alright. Brenda, truth or dare?" Judith asked as she crossed her fingers in hopes that she would pick truth.

"I'll start slow. I'll go with truth," Brenda said, and Judith sighed audibly next to her.

"Why do you think Wheezer killed Betty?" Judith asked slowly.

"Oh, I don't, really. Did you guys think I was serious? I just give her a hard time because she's such a sourpuss, and there's no good gossip around here lately. I need something juicy! A murderer in our midst? That's juicy," Brenda said. "Who's next?"

"I'll go," Jo said. "I pick dare."

"Show us the most embarrassing picture on your phone."

Jo dug around for her phone and pulled up a picture of herself, sleeping, mouth agape, and a string of drool attaching her to the pillow supporting her head. "My lady friend took this of me the other night," she said, with a knowing look at Brenda. Jo looked around the circle of women before her eyes settled on Linda.

"Linda, truth or dare?"

"Oh, truth. Definitely truth," Linda said. Before Jo could ask her question, Judith interrupted.

"Linda, were you ever romantically involved with Betty Black?"

"That's a weird question to ask," Brenda said, but nobody else intervened, so Judith thought she got away with it. But Brenda pressed on. "Ask something more salacious, Jud."

"Alright. Were you ever romantically involved with Betty Black *and,* if you had to, who would you choose to sleep with at this party?

"No, we were just occasional dance partners. She was always a little bit too optimistic for me. I need someone who can handle my obsession with death. And Cynthia is who I would pick. I want to finish what we started at her aphrodisiac party," Linda said and wiggled her eyebrows at Cynthia. "Cynthia, truth or dare?"

"Truth," she replied, winking at Linda. Again, Judith spoke first. "Do you think you've ever gotten so high that you could murder someone and forget it happened?"

"These are terrible questions. Have you ever played this game before? What the hell is wrong with you, Judith? This game is supposed to have sexual undercurrents, not feel like our mom caught us sneaking in from a party. Jesus," Brenda said. "Cynthia, what's the last lie you told?"

"No, Judith, I've never been that high. I don't think anyone's ever been that high. You know, marijuana helps clarity—" Cynthia began, but when she saw everyone's eyes glazing over, she cut herself off. "And the last lie I told is when my daughter asked if I'd smoked weed today. I said no. Helen, truth or dare?"

"Dare!" Helen squealed.

Judith squeezed her shoulder and said, "I knew you'd be daring!"

Elaine rolled her eyes and sighed but managed to keep her mouth shut. She reached over and helped herself to another brownie. They weren't half bad, after all.

"I dare you to do a sexy dance to the song I play," Cynthia said. She scrolled quickly through her list, not wanting to delay the game, and chose "I Want a Little Sugar in My Bowl," by Nina Simone. Helen sashayed until she was directly in front of Judith, and Elaine let out a *for fuck's sake* just under her breath. Her hips bucked, and she slowly unbuttoned her flannel and then wrapped the shirt around Judith's neck. Elaine wished she hadn't noticed what great shape Helen was in; underneath those flannel pajamas was a good-looking lady. Judith smiled gamely and pretended to put a tip into the shoulder strap of her bra.

"Would you look at that?" Hannibird chimed in again.

When the song was finally over, Helen said, "Truth or dare?" to Elaine.

"Dare," Elaine said.

Helen said, "I dare you to eat another brownie."

"I've already had two," Elaine protested.

"That's why it's a dare," Helen challenged.

"Oh, what the hell," Elaine said, and gobbled it up in one enormous bite. She felt very out of sorts, like she was floating somewhere far away.

"Judith, you're up next. Truth or dare?" Elaine asked after she managed to swallow.

"Truth."

"Judith, do you think that, when we yawn, deaf people think we are screaming?" Elaine asked, the brownie evidently having taken affect.

"For the love of Sarah McLachlan, these are not the types of questions fit for a game of Truth or Dare. You've got to ruffle some feathers. Judith, who do you think is the prettiest woman here? Second to Elaine, of course," Brenda asked with an evil grin.

Judith didn't wait quite long enough to answer, in Elaine's opinion.

"Helen, though 'prettiest' isn't the word I would have chosen. Most attractive, maybe. Second-most attractive, I mean," she said with a wink. "But no one compares to the goddess on my left." Judith squeezed Elaine's hand. She decided not to waste the spotlight. "I've got a truth to ask you, Jo."

"But I didn't pick truth—" Jo replied.

"Why did you pick the bathroom lock on the night of Betty's death?"

"Wheezer had to pee. She was cussing and stomping around. I was under threat of urine!" Jo said.

"You sure know how to bring down a mood, Judith. We just saw a striptease! Come on. Elaine, I dare you to undress someone who isn't Judith," Brenda said, determined to stir the pot a bit more.

Elaine still had brownie smudged all around her mouth, but now, it mattered not to her. She didn't know who to pick; she only knew she wanted to make Judith feel a little bit jealous. Was she being childish? Yes. So childish that she had eaten three brownies and was trying to get revenge against the person she loved most in the world. Elaine decided on Brenda, who hadn't yet formed a close bond with Judith but was also quite available. Elaine walked her sexiest walk over toward Brenda, which, at this point, was more of a stumble due to her dizziness. "Brenda, I've got my eye on you," Elaine said in what she hoped sounded like a sultry voice.

"Alright, Cheech, just undress me," Brenda said. Elaine started to pull at the tie on her bathrobe but realized how much sexier it would be if she used her teeth. Kneeling, Elaine got the long end of the tie in her mouth and tried to use her hands to get enough tension to undo the fuzzy bathrobe. Unfortunately, she wasn't coordinated enough at the moment to pull this off. She tried to get more of the bathrobe in her mouth for more leverage and then gagged a little. "Holy hell, Elaine, what are you doing down there? Haven't you encountered a knot before? You're getting brownie all over my nice, white robe."

Giving up, Elaine stood and untied the now wet robe straps with her hands. As she suspected, Brenda was entirely naked underneath, and Brenda was thrilled.

"Now, this is a party!" Brenda squealed. Afterward, judging by everyone's glances, the ladies hoped Brenda would slip her robe back on before the game began again. She did not. Instead, she sat, bare-assed on Judith's kitchen chair.

"Tits, I see tits!" Hannibird clamored.

"Jo, truth or dare," Cynthia said.

"Truth."

"Who is the Secret Pearl traitor who is dating a man?" Cynthia said, looking quite pleased with herself. If Elaine could trust her senses, she thought she saw Jo look helplessly at Brenda before stumbling around for an answer.

"Wow. Is it hot in here?" Jo asked, laughing nervously and wiping her brow. No one flinched, and everyone sat in silent expectance. "Alright, I'll be honest with you. It's...me."

Elaine nearly fell out of her chair.

"You? You would have been the last person I suspected—not just out of the Secret Pearl residents, but of everyone on Earth," Cynthia said.

"Well, it's the truth. I like men, sometimes. I just uh, really, adore their weird, hairy penises and fragile balls. I find it so attractive," Jo choked out the words, convincing no one.

"You told me a while back that you thought dicks looked like a blind sea creature you saw in your nightmares," Linda chortled.

"Yeah, but in a sexy way," Jo replied.

"Alright, I'm not buying it, but it's clear you're not going to give us the real answer," Cynthia said. "What are we doing next?"

"Ouija board. I'm just dying to try it out," Brenda said, seeming overly eager to change the subject. Judith found Cynthia's Ouija board and placed it on the table. Everyone put their fingertips lightly on the planchette, except for Linda and Cynthia.

"I don't mess around with the afterlife. I'm going to be one of these dead souls soon enough, I don't want to piss off any of them," Linda said, getting up to refresh her drink.

"Me either. I'm terrified of my ex trying to communicate with me from the great beyond," Cynthia said.

"But this is your Ouija board, Cynthia," Brenda said.

"I know, and the last time I used it, my ex-husband, who was killed in a car accident a few years back, told me I was a lousy lay. Can you believe that? Me, a lousy lay? He was the one who made me realize I would never enjoy sex with a man!" Cynthia said.

"I didn't know your ex-husband died," Linda said. Cynthia shrugged.

"It was long after we divorced, so I wasn't too broken up about it. I just felt bad for my daughter."

"With whom are we speaking?" Brenda asked in an overly dramatic voice, turning everyone's attention back to the board. The planchette moved slowly. B-E-T-T-Y B-L-A-C-K. "Oh my god! It's Betty, you guys! Betty, what message do you have for us?"

This time the planchette moved more quickly across the board. T-E-L-L J-U-D-I-T-H T-O M-I-N-D H-E-R O-W-N B-U-S-I-N-E-S-S. E-N-O-U-G-H W-I-T-H T-H-E Q-U-E-S-T-I-O-N-S.

"Very funny guys," Judith said and rolled her eyes at Elaine.

"Alright, that's enough fun and games. Let's watch some reruns of *Killing Eve,* shall we?" Jo grabbed the popcorn and made her way to the living room. Brenda followed quickly after, grabbing her hand and giving it a meaningful squeeze. Elaine could just barely make out that she mouthed "thank you," and gave Jo a quick peck on the cheek before the other ladies blocked her view. In the midst of her hazy mood, Elaine realized that, despite her best efforts, she was having a great time.

Chapter Twenty-One

Brenda's Depression Cure

Though the slumber party provided a brief distraction, Brenda had been feeling down for a while after Martina broke up with her. She missed the sex, of course, but she really missed her sexy accent and muscles. Martina had voiced concerns about their relationship not going anywhere, and evidently, Brenda had confirmed them. Usually, Brenda would have called he-who-shall-not-be-named for a round of rebound sex, but after what happened last time with his mother, she decided to become a sex vegetarian—no meat, just bush—for a while, and stick to what she knew best: women. But ever since the breakup, even getting out of bed was a chore.

Jo stopped by for coffee one morning and happened upon Brenda, still in her pajamas at three in the afternoon, lying on her back in the middle of her bedroom, eating graham crackers. Apparently, this was enough information for Jo to diagnose her as "depressed."

"I'm not depressed, Jo, this is my self-care."

"Really? You're taking care of yourself by eating stale snacks that left a crust of crumbs across your skin, with the curtains drawn, in total darkness?"

"Yes."

"I know Martina dumped you, but I'm worried about how hard you're taking this. Did you honestly think you'd be together forever?"

"No, but I much prefer doing the dumping to getting blindsided. I was having so much fun. And she was so young and sexy, but all her energy made me feel old. Old, old, old!"

"If you want more energy, you should go outside. Do you remember sunshine, Brenda? It's good for you. Get some exercise. Take a shower... please. This isn't like you. You need to take care of yourself. This— this is the opposite of self-care. Just looking at you is making me depressed," Jo said, gesturing vaguely at Brenda.

"I like the idea of exercise. And I like having sex with people who get a lot of exercise. But me, exercise? You should know better. I'm betrayed by the mere suggestion, Jo. It's the law of physics or something. Bodies in motion should stay in motion; bodies at rest should stay at rest. I will be fucking with the very fabric of the universe if I exercise."

"Come on, Brenda. I'll go, too. We can do something easy, like yoga."

Grateful to have a friend willing to distract her from her overwhelming sense of nihilism, Brenda agreed. But she would not be attending the sunrise class. No, they would be going after dinner to a night-time yoga session, where no one could see the look on her face when she tore a muscle or split her yoga pants down the middle, a situation she felt was quite likely to occur.

When they got to the class, Jo unrolled her mat and laid on her back, in meditation. Brenda wasn't exactly sure what to do, so she unrolled her mat next to Jo's, and then went to talk to the good-looking instructor at the front of the room.

"Hello, my name is Brenda. I'm new here."

"Hi, Brenda. We practice silence before and after classes, so, unfortunately, I can't chat at the moment."

"Of course, I understand. But I wanted to let you know that your air conditioning seems to be broken. And all these poor ladies on the floor are just sweating up a storm. Could we crack a window or something?"

"I'm sorry, this is hot yoga. We keep the temperature around one-hundred and five degrees throughout the class."

Brenda nodded, embarrassed, and gave Jo a little kick in the side before sitting on her mat.

"Jo, how could you? Hot yoga? In Florida? I feel like I am in the seventh circle of hell!"

A few ladies raised their heads off their mats to shush Brenda.

"Just relax, it will be over in ninety minutes."

"An hour and a half, Jo? I'll be dead by then. You'll have to pay your respects to a Brenda-shaped puddle on the floor."

"Shh!" The instructor had taken notice of their conversation. "Please be respectful and end all conversations before class begins." Brenda decided to quiet down, not wanting to piss off the cute instructor further. Seeing all the attractive people in the room made Brenda grateful that she took a shower, even though her clean hair was already dripping with sweat. After she got used to the heat, she liked the stretching positions. But mostly, she enjoyed seeing the instructor bent in half, demonstrating at the front of the class. When the session finally ended and Jo and Brenda lay in their final savasana, Brenda was sold, though the class was not as easy as Jo had suggested.

"Did you see how sexy the instructor was? I may just become a health nut after this."

"I told you it would be good to get out of the house," Jo said, dabbing at her forehead with a cool, lavender-scented cloth. The instructor made her way over to Brenda and placed her hand on the small of Brenda's back.

"I know this was your first class today, and I just wanted to say how impressed I was with your focus. Every time I glanced at you, you were studying my position so closely, really trying to perfect your posture. You did great!"

Brenda smiled, dug a soggy calling card out of her pocket, and before she knew it, she and the yoga instructor were dating. Her depressive slump had ended as quickly as it began. And Jo felt like she was owed a favor. One morning, over coffee, Jo felt bold enough to mention it.

"Look at you, Brenda. Having coffee with me at ten in the morning, just like old times. And you're not wearing a Halloween candy-stained bathrobe!"

"And I owe it all to you, Jo," Brenda chimed in, just like Jo had hoped.

"Well, you do owe me a little. I got you out of the house when you were depressed, so I was hoping you'd do me a little favor in return."

"Alright, what is it?" Brenda said.

"I think you should have your girlfriend lead a yoga class for the Secret Pearl residents. She's such a good instructor, and she'll do it for you. Plus, everyone will love the view," Jo said with a wink.

"I have been wining and dining her. I am sixty-nining her, too, if you were curious. So I bet she would do it. I'll give her a call."

Brenda was surprised how quickly Virginia, the yoga instructor, agreed to do a free class. She loved to do charity work, something that Brenda was mostly unfamiliar with. Brenda booked the clubhouse and let everyone know about the free candlelight yoga class they were invited to join. When the night of the event came, it was so popular that she had to check with Elaine to ensure that everyone who attended did, in fact, live at the Secret Pearl. There were a few faces she didn't recognize, but Brenda decided to let it slide. She weaved between people to find a place for her mat near all her friends, when she saw Cynthia. Cynthia was barefoot in some leggings and hunched over with her arms dangling limply.

"What on earth are you doing?" Brenda asked.

"I'm trying to touch my toes. Will you let me know when I get close?"

"You're almost to your knees, Cynthia. Stop closing your eyes, and you'll be able to see for yourself," Brenda said.

"But it hurts!" Cynthia said.

Linda was a few mats away, fanning herself intensely.

"I think I'm having a hot flash!" she yelped when she caught Brenda's eye.

"Unless this is a time machine instead of a yoga class, there's no way in hell you are having a hot flash," Brenda retorted. "I turned off the air conditioning to make this more like a hot yoga class, and I have the humidifier turned on high, too. It helps you do some deep stretching."

With nearly overlapping mats and barely enough space to do a downward dog, the class began.

"Welcome, everyone. I'm Virginia, a close personal friend of Brenda's, and she has asked me here today to lead you all in a vinyasa flow. She also asked that the class be taught nude, but I think everyone will be much more comfortable clothed," Virginia said as she made her way to the front of the room.

"That's where you're wrong," Brenda said from the front row. However, what little clothes everyone did wear were form-fitting and minimal, so Brenda decided not to complain too much about the non-nude format. Brenda chose the front row because she thought she at least deserved the best view of Virginia, since she was the one to set up this event. And Virginia looked incredible. She wore a sports bra and yoga pants, and there was nothing between Brenda's eyes and those incredible abs. Come to think of it, Brenda felt sexier than usual, too. She had been regularly attending Virginia's classes, and her newfound flexibility—not yoga-instructor-flexibility, but pretty-damn-good-for-sixty-five flexibility—was something she hoped to show off during the session. It didn't hurt that Jo's mat was directly behind Brenda's.

"We're going to start with child's pose, to help everyone bring their focus to their mats tonight. And then we're going to work up to our climactic pose: tittibhasana, or firefly."

"I don't think I can balance on my titties," Brenda said, unable to practice silence during yoga.

"No, that's just the name: tittibhasana. You'll be balanced on your hands, actually," Virginia said calmly, accustomed to Brenda's occasional outbursts during class.

"Why are we doing hot yoga? Is this punishment for something?" Cynthia asked.

"Any class Virginia teaches is hot yoga, Cynthia," Brenda chimed in again. "It helps you stretch, that's why. You'll like it. Trust me."

"Okay, I'm going to have to ask all of you to quiet down a little, so that we can focus on our intentions. Pick an intention that will serve you throughout your day and guide you for even longer. And then we will move on to the full bind asanas."

"My intention is to peel the yoga teacher out of her clothes as soon as this class is over, and to give a whole new meaning to the term 'full bind,'" Brenda whispered, but not quite quiet enough to avoid Virginia's attention.

"I'm serious, Brenda. No distractions. Now, if any of you don't want me to help correct your yoga pose form, simply place your water bottle on the top right corner of your mat, and I will know not to touch you."

"Where do I place my water bottle if I want you to touch me extra?" Brenda couldn't help herself, it seemed. But the look that Virginia shot her was enough to convince her to keep her mouth closed—at least for a while. When they began doing cat-cow poses, Virginia slipped over to Brenda's mat and gave her an affectionate swat on the behind.

"You behave, Brenda. I'm doing this as a favor to you," Virginia said.

"It's your fault, Virginia. You turn me into a mouthy, disruptive student," Brenda whispered in between stretches.

"And you make me feel like a schoolmaster with a disciplinarian streak. Don't make me institute some kind of corporal punishment," Virginia said, realizing now that the class was staring at her, waiting for the next set of instructions. "Sorry, everyone. Brenda tends to disturb the flow of most of my classes. Well, y'all know her, so I probably don't need to explain."

When class ended, the attendees offered sweaty hugs of appreciation to Brenda and Virginia. After Brenda mopped up her puddle of sweat on the floor, she grabbed her yoga mat and turned to see if Virginia was ready to leave, too.

"I ought to take you over my knee," Virginia said, an impish flicker in her eye.

"You'll do no such thing," Brenda said as she took Virginia's hand to walk back to Brenda's place. "But I'm going to repay you with the hottest sex you've had in quite a while."

Chapter Twenty-Two

———————————●———————————

Going Out with a Bang

Well, Cynthia, I'm planning one more event before I officially retire as the Secret Pearl's social director. I decided I can't let my last event be a failed Christmas party or a slumber party where Judith did all the work. And this event is going to be a doozy. You will have to pick up the reins after that, and I know you'll do a great job," Elaine said, sitting at Cynthia's house on a warm spring morning. Cynthia wandered from plant to plant, sprinkling water on them, and Elaine was wondering how many of these plants were legal in the state of Florida.

"I don't see why we both can't plan events, Elaine. I've always loved your events—most of them, anyway. Dressing up from time to time never killed anyone," Cynthia said, pausing to kneel down and investigate a plant that looked like a lost cause to Elaine. She flicked a crusty leaf onto the floor. "Oh no, I think Herbert is dead," she said gravely.

"I'm not sure that planning events is my thing. And at my age, I've got to find out what my thing is—the sooner, the better. I'll drag Judith to a charity gala once a year to get my fill of extravagance and fashion. Your events are better for the Secret Pearl gang, and I've come to terms with that," Elaine said, refilling her coffee cup.

"Help me lift this," Cynthia said, struggling with Herbert's large, white pot. "I've got to bury him in the backyard." *So that explains why her backyard is full of dead plants,* thought Elaine.

"You know these might stand a fighting chance if you buried them

131

in the backyard right off the bat, Cynthia. Indoor plants aren't as much of a necessity in Florida as they are in Colorado."

"Shh, I don't want Herbert's last moments to be him hearing you accusing me of his murder. Anyway, what kind of event are you planning? A white-tie evening soiree? A silent auction? Some sort of garden party spectacular?"

"No, I'm planning the annual dance at the clubhouse. And guess what: there will be line-dancing. Beer, too," Elaine said.

"Well, everyone is going to love it. And you can have the 'Official Party Planner of the Secret Pearl' title back any time you want it," Cynthia said. The two women successfully buried Herbert in the backyard, amongst others with grey-brown leaves, starved of sunlight and giving the outdoor space an abandoned look. When they had finished, Cynthia jotted down the party details on her calendar, and Elaine left to invite the others. Her friends had warmed to her events, especially since the last one—the investigation disguised as a slumber party—had been such a success. It seemed everyone would attend her final soiree, and this was an enormous relief to Elaine. She would go out with a bang.

The night of the party arrived, and everyone came, just as Elaine had hoped. Even Wheezer made an appearance, much to everyone's surprise, and she was decked out in head to toe western wear, including jeans, boots, and a cowboy hat. For a moment, the ladies stared at her—they hadn't seen her since her time in jail—but Linda and Elaine rushed right over.

"Welcome, Wheezer! I'm so glad you came. I didn't think you'd show up after Cynthia's brunch incident," Elaine said. She showed Linda and Wheezer over to the appetizers and drinks table. "Everything is shrimp-free, Linda, and Brenda brought her bean dip. I even bought six different types of beer, so you should be able to find something you like." Elaine was clearly pleased with herself, and the clubhouse buzzed with vibrant music and energy.

"Not a truffle or pâté in sight. Good job, Elaine! I'm almost sorry you won't be planning these shindigs anymore," Linda said, filling a plate with snacks.

"Let's just hope all the excitement doesn't kill someone," Wheezer said.

"So did your time in the clink change you, Wheezer? What was it like being behind bars?" Linda's eagerness to hear about the drama was written all over her face.

"Well, those seventy-two hours were the longest of my life. I came out of that hellhole angry, bitchy, and unable to suffer anyone's bullshit with a smile. So, no, I wouldn't say it changed me."

Linda snorted in response.

"We missed you. It's not the same Secret Pearl without you around, Wheezer," Linda said. Elaine decided to let the two friends catch up on recent events and went to search for Judith. "Boot Scootin' Boogie" came over the speakers, and most of the partygoers filled in the dance floor. As the crowd parted, Elaine found Judith opening a bottle of wine with Helen, talking and laughing. She rolled her eyes and made her way over to them.

"I'm going to need you to share that wine," Elaine said, and Judith immediately intuited why she was annoyed.

"Elaine, Helen brought a special bottle that she's been saving for years for me to try. Isn't that the sweetest thing you've ever heard?" Judith gushed.

"You're welcome to have some, too, Elaine. But why aren't you out on the dance floor with everyone else?" Helen said as she deftly uncorked the dusty bottle. Elaine interpreted this as Helen trying to get rid of her, to spend some more precious moments with Judith alone.

"I don't know how to do the Boot Scootin' Boogie, of course. I've never line danced in my life," Elaine said, trying to calm her voice.

"Are you serious? You shouldn't even be allowed to have a Florida address if you've never been boot scootin'. Come on; I'll teach you. Judith, there better be some of this bottle left by the end of the song," Helen said, grabbing Elaine's hand and leading her out to the dance floor. Fortunately, the line dance wasn't too complicated, and Elaine picked it up after several measures. Helen gave her an earnest thumbs up, and Elaine began to relax and realized she was having fun in spite of herself. Maybe Helen wasn't trying to corner her girlfriend after all. Maybe Helen was a lot of fun and had much in common with both Elaine and Judith. Elaine felt like a jerk. When the song wound down, she pulled Helen close enough to whisper.

"Thanks for forcing me to have some fun. I mean it. I would have never given it a shot if you hadn't dragged me up there. There's even a chance line dancing is something I could appreciate in small doses," Elaine said.

Judith was waiting for them with a full glass of red for each of them. "Cheers," she said, gently clinking their glasses together. "This bottle of red is older than my oldest cat by a long shot!" she exclaimed, examining the Silver Oak bottle.

Elaine and Judith agreed the wine was sublime but hesitated to venture any tasting notes in front of the sommelier. When Helen described it as tasting of cassis and forest undergrowth, they both nodded sagely without having any idea what cassis or forest undergrowth tasted like, or why Helen found the tastes familiar. All too quickly, the wine was gone, and Judith was leading Elaine to the clubhouse bathroom.

"What's the matter, dear? Want me to get the stool softener? I brought some in my purse, just in case," Elaine said, unzipping a small compartment in her designer bag.

"No, no. I just saw you line dancing and had to have you," Judith said, leading Elaine into the fateful bathroom.

"You want to have sex in here? At the scene of the crime?" Elaine said louder than she meant to.

"It's the only place we can get a little privacy," Judith pleaded. "You just look so good in your boots and denim mini skirt. And you made line dancing look so sexy. I've never seen you looking this country-fied before." Judith bit her lip, and Elaine didn't stand a chance putting her off another minute.

"Well, I did take ballet lessons for a few years as a little girl," Elaine said while Judith tore off her skirt. Judith saw that Elaine was wearing her favorite pair of black silk panties and gave her an excited smile. Judith pulled Elaine's panties down her legs, around her boots, and stuffed them in her pocket. No romance or foreplay was in store for Elaine this time; Judith's hands found the most sensitive spots on Elaine's body in a matter of moments. It felt good, but Elaine was distracted.

"I hate to tell you, Jud, but I've never been able to come in public."

"We're not in public," Judith said somewhat incomprehensibly, not bothering to pause for the chitchat.

"We're in a *public* bathroom," Elaine said. "It feels amazing; I just didn't want you to think it was your skills preventing me—it's just me and my inhibitions."

"Uhm-hhm." After a few moments, Judith's lust had calmed down a bit, and Elaine had enjoyed herself thoroughly. "We can rejoin the party, now, if you want," Judith said. Elaine was torn. She loved indulging Judith's spontaneous side, but she also didn't want to miss too much of her last party. Judith had promised Elaine at least one slow dance, and Elaine had been looking forward to it all day. They freshened themselves up briefly before gingerly opening the door. Just outside, Wheezer was waiting, exasperated.

"Finally! Jesus, what was the holdup? I almost peed on the goddamn floor. For a minute, I assumed someone else was dying in here again. Wait a minute; I think I know what the holdup was," Wheezer said, giving the couple an accusatory look. Wheezer disappeared into the restroom, and the two women blushed.

"I can't believe we got caught!" Judith said.

"I feel like I'm in high school again, sneaking behind the bleachers," Elaine said with a laugh. A slow song poured through the speakers, and Elaine talked Judith into a dance before the party was over.

"I can't believe my luck. Moving here, meeting you, making so many new friends. I feel like this is the start of something big," Judith said, resting her head on Elaine's shoulder. But before Elaine could respond, the song was cut short. She saw Wheezer on the stage, tapping the microphone, and getting everyone's attention.

"Before I leave this party—which, thanks to Elaine, is the most fun I've had in a while—I want to make a quick announcement. Betty's family gave us a small share of her ashes in an urn to add to our collection on the mantle here since the Secret Pearl was such an important part of her extended family. I wanted to have a moment of silence for Betty as she joins those who have gone before us on the mantle," Wheezer said, her voice a little shaky. Wheezer placed the small, yellow urn on the mantle, kissed her fingertips, and touched the top of it. After a few moments, she returned to the stage. "Thank you, everyone."

Helen raised her glass of wine up high. "To Betty!"

"To Betty!" Everyone replied in bittersweet cheers. Only a few feet behind Elaine and Judith, Brenda was already firing up the gossip mill.

"Am I the only one who thinks it's a bit suspicious that Wheezer had Betty's ashes?" she said with a knowing look.

"Yes, Brenda. You're making so much sense. Not only did I kill her, but when the cops weren't looking, I stole her corpse, burned it, and then publicly announced that I kept her ashes, just to avoid any further suspicion. Do you honestly think her family would entrust me with a portion of her ashes if I were still a person of interest?" Wheezer said, surprising Brenda with her proximity. Wheezer grabbed Elaine and Judith's arms. "Come on, guys, there's something I need to tell you."

Chapter Twenty-Three

———————•———————•———————

Wheezer Spills the Beans

The three women walked briskly over to Wheezer's place as Judith and Elaine exchanged quizzical glances about what Wheezer could possibly have to tell them.

"I think you two are the only sane ones here—and I think you believe I am innocent. I want to tell you what happened the night Betty died, but I don't want to do it anywhere near Brenda. She misconstrues everything. That woman has such a grudge against me, and for the life of me, I don't know why." Wheezer pulled a set of keys out of her pocket and led the women inside.

"Wow, your place is so elegant, Wheezer. This is without a doubt the first time I've ever seen it," Elaine said, and Wheezer raised her eyebrows.

"Do you want a glass of wine? What I'm about to tell you is kind of intense," Wheezer continued, ignoring the awkward compliment and pulling out barstools for them to sit on before she rummaged through her kitchen cabinets.

"You know I'm always up for some red," Judith said, and Elaine nodded that she would have a glass, too. Wheezer poured some wine into three glasses and focused her penetrating gaze on Judith and Elaine.

"As far as I know, I was the last person to see Betty alive, and the first person to see her dead. But I didn't kill her; I swear it," Wheezer said, before taking a small sip of wine.

"Okay, you can't stop there. We have to hear the whole story," Elaine said, unable to hold her excitement back.

"First of all, you should know that Betty and I dated a while back. It wasn't serious for her, but it was quite serious for me. We kept it pretty private; I'm always private with my romantic life. Anyway, on the night of the party, we were getting along, and you know what a rarity that is for me, getting along with someone. She told me that she wanted to have sex with me in the bathroom, that it was something that was on her bucket list. So, I agreed, and we did. When I left the bathroom, she was fine! I swear on my life that she was fine. But then when I had to pee about a half an hour later, Jo busted the door down, and I was as surprised as anyone to find that she was still in there, dead."

"You had sex with her on the toilet?" Elaine said, shooting a disgusted look at Wheezer.

"You don't get to judge me anymore, honey. I know what you did in there tonight," Wheezer said with a laugh. "Anyway, I didn't want to tell anyone we had just had sex since I thought everyone would find it all the more suspicious. Either someone else went in there and killed her after I left, or she just died. I don't know how or why, but sometimes, people suddenly die."

"I believe you, Wheezer. I want to get more evidence so that we can clear you for good. But I'm not even sure where to start. Her family cleaned her place out a few months ago," Judith said, pacing back and forth across Wheezer's kitchen floor as she gestured out her window, where Betty had lived across the street. "So, I'm sure there's nothing left to look for there. If only we had access to her cellphone or something that would prove you two were fond of each other."

"We hadn't been texting back and forth lately, if that's what you mean. But I might have an idea. It's not strictly legal though, or moral, or ethical, and I don't want you two to get on my case about it," Wheezer said.

"Go on. I'm not here to judge! I mean, not anymore," Elaine said.

"I might have Betty's email password."

"Might?" Judith asked.

"Well, I did as of a few years ago. I haven't checked to see if it still works, but she gave it to me when we were dating, to assure me she wasn't cheating on me. Good lord, I was such a head case when we were dating. Anyway, we could see if there were emails from anyone who had a bone to pick with her," Wheezer said, searching the two ladies' faces for any trace of critical, goody-goody expressions.

Judith didn't miss a beat.

"I say we go for it. The Medical Examiner has completely dropped the ball, and Wheezer, you're still taking the heat around here for something you didn't do. Betty isn't around anymore, so we're not technically invading her privacy. I'm all for it."

The women gathered around the glow of Wheezer's laptop as she typed in the username: YellowPolkaDotsLesbyterian, and then the password.

"Her fucking password is 'password'—or, at least, it was. I cannot believe her identity never got stolen," Wheezer said while waiting for the screen to load. "Well, it worked! We're in. So, what the hell do we do now? I don't know what to look for. Any suggestions, Nancy Drew?"

Elaine and Judith shrugged, so Wheezer glanced through the most recent emails. Most were updates from food sites about the latest baking recipes or must-have tools that Betty probably would have bought with money she didn't have, if she were still here, Wheezer thought. Scrolling down further, they saw an email from her sister confirming a plan to visit for a weekend that never happened due to the unfortunate circumstances.

"Let's check her 'sent' folder," Judith suggested. The most recently sent message was titled, "Refill Request," and sent to contactus@ gulfcoasthealthcenters.com. "Click that one!" Judith said, so excited that she almost spilled her drink. They read the email together in silence.

> Hi, Doctor Cox,
> I've been so busy lately that I forgot to request my refill in advance. Can you please send a new prescription over to my pharmacy on Bayview Drive at your earliest convenience? I'm completely out of my beta blockers and nitroglycerin tabs. I know, I know, you told me last time I ran out that I can never run out of these again. But, I forgot, and here we are. Thanks, doc!
> Betty the Forgetty

"What the hell are beta blockers?" Wheezer asked before Elaine could. "Judith, you should know since you were a veterinarian."

"Well, for animals, you can use nitroglycerin as a vasodilator to treat congestive heart failure. And beta blockers are another cardiac medication."

"You're saying she had a bad heart?" Wheezer asked, tears springing to her eyes and an unexpected pang of guilt gripping her chest. *Why didn't she go to the emergency room? Why didn't she tell me she had a condition? Why, oh why, did I have sex with her in the bathroom,* Wheezer thought, trying to contain herself.

"Well, that pretty much proves it. You didn't kill her, Wheezer. I have a few calls to make in the morning," Judith said, and the two women left Wheezer to a new wave of grief.

Chapter Twenty-Four

Betty's Bucket List

Betty twirled the phone cord around her fingers and adjusted her posture on the kitchen chair. She always sat in the one without the bright cushion, because she left those for guests, even when she was home alone. But the hard wood of the chair wasn't comfortable for the long, twice-per-week phone conversations with her sister.

"That's why you never marry a man, Daisy," Betty said after listening to her younger sister complain without taking a breath for five minutes straight.

"Well, I'm seventy, Betty. I'm fairly sure it's too late for me to cross over to the other side now. Is it honestly easier for me to give women a try than it is for Dirk to do the fucking dishes once in his life?" Daisy said, her voice rising to a shout again. Betty wondered if Dirk was in earshot, as he commonly was when Daisy was having these heart-to-hearts with her.

"Sorry to hear it, Daisy. I can't say I have any advice to give you. My love life is in shambles, too. Don't worry, though, no worse than usual. I haven't spoken to Dana in two weeks. I'm not sure if she's just taking some time to calm down or if it's really over this time. I guess I called her Wheezer in my sleep again." Betty could hear Daisy snort on the other end of the line.

"You and your sleep talking. I don't know how anyone puts up with it. I would have left you, too! Calling out someone else's name in bed—that's a cardinal sin."

"Sin, schmin, I forfeited any chance I had of making it into heaven a long time ago. And it's not like we were doing anything in bed, sis, I was just asleep. I don't even know why it happened," Betty said, pushing back an errant cuticle on her right hand. She looked at the back of her hand in disbelief; surely this was her mother's hand and not her own. It was bony and covered in age spots and thin skin. No matter what she tried, her age always showed on her hands.

"That's almost worse. Were you dreaming about her? Is she stuck in your subconscious?"

"Oh, hell, I don't know. All I know is Dana woke me up in a rage and started packing her things. Maybe she dreamed it; I have no recollection of it at all."

"You do talk in your sleep—we both know that. You should apologize. Hang on, Betty. Dirk needs something urgently, I think. What's that, Dirk? Get yourself a damn sandwich!" Betty heard Daisy yell away from the receiver to Dirk, who had no idea how much trouble he was in. "Hey, you should plan to spend a weekend with us sometime. It's been too long. I'm starting to forget what your wrinkly old face looks like."

"My face might be old, but you know it's not wrinkly. I'm having my next tune-up with Doctor Jason in two weeks, so I'll look as plump and dewy as a baby's bum. Anyway, I can't do it this weekend. I have a thing, some sort of event I got roped into. It's not even line-dancing, so I have no idea why I agreed to go. It's some sort of a wine-tasting thing. Anyway, Wheezer will be there, so I'm going to see if I can get my Botox moved up so that she can see what she's missing."

"You and your tune-ups. You look beautiful as ever, sis. You don't need it. And anyway, you crazy lesbos know nothing about child-rearing. A baby's bum shouldn't be dewy; you have to keep it bone dry, or that poor kid will have a nasty case of diaper rash."

"Whatever you say, sis. Maybe the weekend after. Let me check my calendar," Betty said and thumbed lazily through her junk drawer looking for her pocket calendar. She saw her prescription bottle and vaguely remembered leaving it by her calendar so that she would order some more. She picked it up and gave it a gentle shake—it was empty. "Oh, crap, Daisy. I have to go. I forgot to have my doctor renew my prescriptions, and I'm completely out."

"Are you kidding? Again? I'm worried about you. You have to start taking this stuff more seriously. You're not a spring chicken anymore—you can't just do whatever you want without conseq—"

"Love you, bye!" Betty said, hanging up the phone. Every so often these days, she forgot one thing or another. She hadn't worried about it in the past, but the things she neglected now were becoming more and more critical. For one thing, she couldn't remember why on earth she had ended things with Wheezer. Maybe that was why she was dreaming about it. Of course, Betty had always loved playing the field, but usually, she had a good enough head on her shoulders not to let something good slip away. And now, the meds. Betty hadn't meant to hang up on her sister, but she was a little worried if she didn't get in touch with her doctor at that very moment, she would forget again.

Then, there was a ring from her doorbell, and Brenda appeared at her door wearing something shamelessly low cut for ten in the morning on a Tuesday.

"Hello, darling. I heard you and Dana called it quits. Want to have some rebound sex this weekend? I've got a night open with your name on it," Brenda said, entering her home without quite being invited.

"Oh, that sounds nice, Brenda, but I'm not sure I'm up for it this time. Dana and I are on a break, I think. It's not officially over. And I've been doing some reflecting, and I might not even be over Wheezer yet. My love life is too complicated for a rebound these days."

"Wheezer, oh my god, Wheezer? You and Wheezer?" Brenda looked like the wind had been knocked out of her.

"Yeah, it was brief and it happened a long time ago, but it was intense," Betty replied calmly. Brenda took a deep breath and shook her head, trying to shake away the visual of Betty and Wheezer together.

"Well, the best place to heal is in another lover's arms," Brenda said, flashing Betty a dazzling smile and batting her long eyelashes.

"I hate to turn you down, but it's not happening. Not this time. I just need to figure out exactly what I want. I don't know how much time I have left, and I've been making bad decisions lately. I need some time to clear my head."

"Ugh, Wheezer. I can't even imagine it; it's too horrible. Wheezer is mean, Betty, and you're so pretty and pleasant and spontaneous. And you know we had better sex together than the two of you ever did," Brenda said.

"Actually, that's not true, Brenda. She meant something to me. I don't think you even know her that well, Brenda, to be casting all those aspersions. She's funny, and she's caring. Wheezer and I had a connection like nothing I've ever experienced in my life. And I ended it so I could have my freedom. It seems so silly now. But it was the best sex of my life," Betty said, feeling anxiety rise as she saw the look on Brenda's face.

"So you're telling me that the sex you had with Wheezer was better than sex you had with me? I won't hear it, and I won't believe it! I will not be insulted like this, Betty. You take that back. You take it back, now. I'm the best lay in this whole goddamn manufactured housing community, and you know it!"

"Before Wheezer, I would have agreed with you, Brenda. But I think I loved Wheezer," Betty said, surprised that steam wasn't coming out of Brenda's ears.

"I have never been this humiliated in my entire life!" Brenda said, standing and turning to leave.

"Oh, Brenda, don't be petty. I would have never said anything— but you brought it up."

"Look, missy. You have to be petty to be a lawyer. It's practically a requirement. Lawyers do not take rejection very well, and you better believe you're going to regret this. You just lost the best no-strings-attached hookup of your life," Brenda said, rushing for the door.

"Once you calm down, let's have coffee," Betty said, but Brenda was stomping off, and she couldn't tell whether or not Brenda heard her. She sat back down at the kitchen table and shook her head as she replayed Brenda's overreaction in her mind. But then she realized she had something she needed to do; something important, she was sure of it. Damn it, this was why her sister always told her to keep a little notebook in her pocket with her to-do list on it. It was so unnerving, this feeling that one moment she had control over a thought, and the next, it would disappear completely like water slipping through her fingers. Was she supposed to pick a date to visit Daisy? No, she couldn't, the wine-tasting was coming up this weekend. Maybe she would just send her an email with some dates that might work. And then she remembered: she needed to move up the appointment with Doctor Jason for Botox so that she looked absolutely stunning when she saw Wheezer again. She sighed with relief as she got her phone out and dialed the familiar number.

When the night of the party came, Betty glanced in the mirror one last time before gathering her purse and heels to head out. She looked unbelievable. No one in their right mind would guess her age, that's for sure. She easily looked fifteen years younger than she was, and she fit into a dress that she'd bought two years ago hoping she'd eventually summon the willpower to go on a diet. Betty felt sexy and ready to rub it in Wheezer's face.

As Betty entered the clubhouse, she saw that Wheezer was standing alone by the snacks, as she often did during social gatherings like this.

"Wheezer, nice to see you," Betty said, as coolly as she could muster.

"Same to you," Wheezer said, not even making eye contact. "Where's your date?"

"Oh, I don't have a date right now. Dana and I are taking a break. What about you?"

"I never bring a date to these things. I only come for the free booze. And honestly, this is a little too fancy to me, so I think I'm going to take off. If I wanted people drinking wine they can't afford to judge me for being alone, I'd have gone to visit my parents more often."

"Don't go just yet, Wheezer. I was hoping we could catch up," Betty said, wondering how the conversation had gotten away from her. Wheezer seemed angry already, and Betty felt like she was losing the battle. "I had a dream about you. That's why Dana's mad at me. She's the one who said we needed to take a break. Well, she didn't so much say it as pack up her things and leave. I guess I was talking about you in my sleep."

"Really? Well, the mind does curious things, I suppose. You never can tell when rubbish from the past is going to get dredged up again," Wheezer said, still not smiling.

"I just miss you. That's what I'm trying to say," Betty said, hoping that Wheezer wouldn't use her vulnerability against her, as she was so prone to doing.

"I'm not surprised. You always want what you can't have. When you were with me, you wanted your freedom. Now you have your freedom, so it makes sense you want me. I'd get a therapist if I were you," Wheezer said.

"Come on, Wheezer, don't be like that. I know I messed up. I want you to give me another chance. I feel like I can't trust my mind anymore. I made all these purchases I don't even remember making. And I've spent so much time racking my brain, trying to figure out why I couldn't make it work with you. I never have a good reason for how things turned out between us."

"I'm not going to give you another chance while you have Dana waiting in the wings, honey. I'm tired of playing second fiddle to everyone else in the world who would just love to get their shot with you," Wheezer crossed her arms, and Betty realized she was right. She unzipped her purse and pulled out her phone.

"Okay, watch," Betty typed out a quick but final breakup text message to Dana. "You can push send."

"Oh, no, you don't. If this is what you want, go for it. But I'm not guaranteeing anything is going to happen between us," Wheezer said, but Betty detected a ray of hope in Wheezer's eyes as she pushed the button. Betty grabbed Wheezer's hand, and Wheezer didn't snatch it back. "Have you met the new resident? Judith?" Wheezer asked after a few moments passed.

"Oh, she must be who moved in across the street," Betty said.

"She's naïve but friendly enough," Wheezer said over the din of the wine-tasting instructions. "You know how you always said having sex in public was on your bucket list?"

Betty smiled. Wheezer wasn't so stubborn after all.

"Yes. What are you thinking?"

"I just saw the bathroom is vacant. Want to go in there and make up for some lost time?"

Betty's heart began pounding out of her chest so hard that she truly felt it might burst. She couldn't believe her luck. Everything was turning out just how she had hoped.

"Yes, Wheezer, that's exactly what I want," Betty said. She felt like a schoolgirl again, dizzy and almost faint at the prospect of reuniting with her sweetheart. She squeezed Wheezer's hand, and the two made their way into the bathroom.

"You first or me first," Wheezer asked, putting their belongings on the little shelf and unbuttoning her blouse.

"I'd love to be a better sport about this, but I have a nasty pain right in my jaw, Wheez. It just sprung up out of nowhere," Betty said, wincing as she rubbed the spot where her ears, neck, and jaw met. She probably should have taken an aspirin—something her doctor liked her to do anyway because of her heart condition. Oh, crap, her cardiologist, she suddenly remembered. How long had it been since she took her medication? Well, she could take an aspirin for now, and email her doctor quickly. She would probably be fine. She felt fine. Hell, she felt better than she had since she and Wheezer broke up. "Hang on, Wheezer, I have to send a quick email," Betty said as she took out her phone and swallowed a dry aspirin.

"Really?" Wheezer said, looking a bit impatient. But then she seemed to think better of her chastisement and calmed herself down. She took a deep breath and smiled. "I have been looking forward to this ever since we broke up."

Betty slipped out of her dress, her heart racing with Wheezer standing before her. Wheezer still knew exactly what to do, remembered exactly what she liked. It took only a few minutes before she felt the anticipation—and then the inevitability—of orgasm. It felt so overwhelming, so amazing, but the rush of calm after the climax never descended. Her heart still felt like she was in the throes of passion, and her head felt foggy, strange.

"You okay? I'll take a rain check—you can get me next time," Wheezer said, buttoning up.

"I'm sorry. I mean, thank you. Just give me a minute to freshen up," Betty said, and she sat on the toilet with a smile on her face as she watched Wheezer walk away.

Chapter Twenty-Five

Here We Go Again

H ello, this is Judith. I'd like to speak to the Medical Examiner, please. Yes, I'll hold," Judith said, holding her cell phone up to her ear, Clawdia on her lap, and Elaine in her eyesight, dressed only in a towel after her shower. "Hi, my name is Judith Fletcher. I have reason to believe that one of the post-mortems in your backlog may have had to do with a heart condition. Is that something you'd be able to double-check for me?"

"Ma'am, we don't take suggestions for causes of death—especially from people who aren't in the field. But I can see if we have finished up the examination you're talking about. Can I have a first and last name?"

"Yes: Betty Black. She died several months ago, and we've been waiting to hear if there was foul play. She was a resident over here at the Secret Pearl, and we just want to give everyone some peace of mind." Judith heard silence on the other end.

"That case has been wrapped up for months, ma'am. Months. We may be behind schedule, but we're not that behind," the voice said.

"Alright, where can I talk to someone about the results?"

"We sent it over to Officer Hank Taylor four months ago—I'd check with him. We're not exactly supposed to discuss these things, HIPAA and all that. But he can confirm whether or not there was foul play."

"I just saw Officer Hank a couple of weeks ago, and he said he'd never gotten the report," Judith said, her brow crinkling.

"Man, I hate that guy," the voice said. "I suggest calling him again. He is so slow. You have to be a real idiot to be as bad of a cop as Hank." Click.

"Son of a bitch! Son of a bitch!" Hannibird squawked.

"You always know what I'm thinking, Hannibird," Judith said. She was combing through the notes in her purse, looking for Officer Hank's business card. "Honey? Do you have Officer Hank's phone number? I can't seem to find it." Elaine was in the other room, getting ready for the day, or, more specifically, their date that night. They had it marked on the calendar for a few weeks now: tonight was tie-me-to-the-bed night at last.

"No, I threw it away immediately. That guy was a piece of work. I only kept his partner's number—he seemed more competent. Officer... Jeremy, was it?" Elaine put down her hairdryer and went to her purse to rifle through her collection of business cards. "Here you go."

"I just talked to the Medical Examiner's Office, and they said Betty's autopsy report was completed months ago."

"Somehow, I'm not surprised," Elaine said, turning the hairdryer back on.

"We have to call him. I want Wheezer off the hook, once and for all," Judith yelled over the roar of the hairdryer before dialing. "Yes, hi, my name is Judith Fletcher, and I'd like to speak with Officer Jeremy."

Judith found herself thankful that there was only one 'Jeremy' employed by their local police department, and she waited with bated breath to talk to him.

"Hello, Jeremy. This is Judith from the Secret Pearl—you recently investigated Betty Black's death. She died on the toilet—I'm sure you remember. Anyway, I hate to involve myself in your affairs, but I spoke with the Medical Examiner, and they said they gave Officer Hank the report months ago. Would you be able to check on this?"

An exhausted sigh was all she heard on the line.

"Yes, of course. Hank, get in here! Hank? Hank, the M.E. office said they gave you the Betty Black report months ago. Have you been slacking on managing the inbox on your desk?"

Straining to listen, Judith could hear a small voice on the other end of the line.

"No, sir. I always deal with my inbox immediately."

"So, you saw the report? Damn it, Hank, we need to close this case."

"No, sir. I didn't read it. As soon as I get some mail in my inbox, I put it into a box. Isn't that what an inbox is for?"

"Jesus, Hank. You have to open your mail."

"Oh, I always open my mail. I even have a pen pal," she heard Hank say, and she cracked a smile.

"Not your personal mail, you doofus. The mail you get here at work! You have to open it and read it. Get rid of your boxes and start sorting your mail. There's time-sensitive stuff in there! Sorry, ma'am, I meant to put you on mute. Hank is checking right now." After a silent moment, she heard Hank yelling with glee.

"I found it! It says Betty Black died of natural causes related to her coronary artery disease. She had a heart attack. Jeremy, I solved my first case!"

"Ma'am, she died of natural causes. Sorry that you had to follow up on this. Thanks for calling," Jeremy said before ending the call. Judith went into her bedroom, where Elaine was choosing an outfit from the small selection of clothes that now lived permanently in Judith's closet.

"She died of natural causes, Elaine. I'm calling everyone over to make the announcement!"

Once all the women filled her living room, it was Hannibird who captured their attention. Perched on Judith's shoulder, he said, "Shut the fuck up! Shut the fuck up," until the side conversations were quelled.

"Thanks for coming, everyone. I thought this was important enough that I should get you all together to give you an update on Betty's death. I wanted you to hear the information from me so that no more rumors get started. Brenda, I'm talking to you. We spoke with the Medical Examiner's office and the police department this morning, and Betty's death was from a heart attack. She died naturally. No one murdered her, and I think we all owe Wheezer a big apology," Judith said.

"Oh, thank goodness," Wheezer said. "No need for an apology. I know that I was the last one to see her, and that's why you all suspected me."

"You were the last one to see her?" Brenda asked.

"Well, yes. Betty pulled me into the bathroom for a quick tryst during the party. We had dated a while back, though we were pretty private about it, and I think she wanted to reconcile. Believe me, I had no idea she had a heart condition," Wheezer said.

"You fucked her to death!" Brenda said triumphantly.

"No, no. She was alive when I left—and happy. I think it must have happened sometime after that," Wheezer said.

"What a way to go," Brenda said. "I hope I'm so lucky. Living it up until the very last minute. Wheezer, if I ever get diagnosed with something terminal, promise me that you'll take me to the bathroom, too, and put me out of my misery."

"What were her last words, Wheezer?" Cynthia asked.

"I believe she said she was going to freshen up. Nothing too preachy, which was fitting for Betty, I think," Wheezer said.

"No doubt my last word in life will be 'fuck.' I'm a lady like that," Jo said.

"Well, I may not be on my deathbed yet, but I'm probably next. I've got a rash like you wouldn't believe, and all signs point to my imminent demise. And I want my epitaph to read: 'I told you I was sick,'" Linda said, "just like that headstone we saw when we walked around the Key West cemetery during Fantasy Fest."

"I want my exit to be at least as dramatic as Betty's—maybe more so. I want it to be just like Juliet and Juliet," Brenda said.

"What the hell is Juliet and Juliet?" Jo asked.

"Oh, it's the lesbian porno version of Romeo and Juliet. I have it if you'd like to borrow it, but believe me, it gets sad at the end," Brenda said.

"I just want to go quickly, in my sleep, with a loved one at my side," Elaine said, winking at Judith.

"I want my death to fulfill some ancient prophecy or signal the end of days. Or I could see myself dying in a heroic karate battle. Either way," Jo said.

Wheezer rolled her eyes. "I'm just glad this fiasco is over. I want things to get back to normal at the Secret Pearl—well, at least as normal as they ever are."

"I think this might be the most morbid gathering I've ever been to," Elaine said, hoping to instigate a subject change.

"That reminds me. When is the next event you're planning? I want to put it on my calendar." Jo pulled a pen from behind her ear and fetched a notebook out of her back pocket.

"I'm taking a step back from event planning, ladies. Cynthia's going to be in charge now. I'm positive that she's going to do a great job, and that every single one of us will accidentally get high between now and next year," Elaine said with a chuckle.

"Wow, you've got some fancy shoes to fill, Cynthia," Jo said.

"That's right. You better buckle the fuck up, because Cynthia Chen is in charge of parties from now on. And I'm going to knock your socks off. Also, if you have any ideas, let me know, because my mind has been kind of fuzzy lately and I haven't been able to think of anything," Cynthia said, twisting her hemp bracelet between her fingers.

"Hey guys," Helen said, looking out Judith's window. "Women are moving into Betty's old place." Outside the window, a U-Haul had parked in her driveway, and unloading boxes were a couple of gals who looked to be in their fifties. They looked happy and sweet, and they probably had no idea about the amateur murder investigation that had preceded the house's vacancy.

"Here we go again," Wheezer said. The ladies filed out the door to meet the newbies and induct them into life at Secret Pearl.

Follow, share, like, and comment at:
www.facebook.com/authorjcmorgan

P.S. It means the world to me that you read my book. Writing is a passion for me, and I look forward to your feedback.
If you liked this book, I'd like to ask for a small favor. Would you be so kind as to leave a review? It would be very much appreciated...
From your friend, J.C. Morgan
Hope to see you again soon!

Made in the USA
Las Vegas, NV
29 August 2021